Join Xena as sh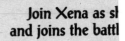
and joins the battl

The exciting exploits of Xena: Warrior Princess

THE EMPTY THRONE
PROPHECY OF DARKNESS
THE THIEF OF HERMES
THE HUNTRESS AND THE SPHINX

Prophecy of Darkness

A novel by
Stella Howard

Based on the Universal television series
created by
John Schulian and Robert Tapert

HarperCollins*Publishers*

This novel is entirely a work of fiction.
The names, characters and incidents portrayed in it are
the work of the author's imagination. Any resemblance to
actual persons, living or dead, events or localities is
entirely coincidental

HarperCollins*Publishers*
77–85 Fulham Palace Road,
Hammersmith, London W6 8JB

A Paperback Original 1997
1 3 5 7 9 8 6 4 2

First published in the USA by Boulevard Books 1997

A catalogue record for this book
is available from the British Library

ISBN 0 00 651149 X

Set in Trump Medieval

Printed and bound in Great Britain by
Caledonian International Book Manufacturing Ltd, Glasgow

For my mother, Dianne—who showed me what
it means to be a true warrior.

1

The small fire crackled and popped, sending tiny sparks into the gathering night. Dark trees bowed and swayed in the mild, early summer breeze, the air rich with the scent of pine and sun-warmed earth.

Gabrielle sat back from her efforts, watching the tiny flames lick against the twigs and branches she had gathered. The fire had to burn down before they could cook anything, at least another twenty minutes—and then it would still take time to roast the rabbit Xena had found for dinner. Gabrielle sighed, then glanced over at her companion. Xena sat cross-legged behind her, her back against a stone, her sword in her lap. The dark-haired warrior was inspecting the blade carefully, her sharp, icy eyes searching for nicks and dull spots.

1

"I'm starving," said Gabrielle, then she sighed again. "I wish we still had some of that jerky from the last village."

Xena didn't look up from her examination. The blade was fine, as it had been the night before—but she never neglected her daily check; the quality of a sword would often decide the outcome of a battle, and a blade could never be too sharp. She'd learned a long time ago that if she took care of her weapons, they would take care of her.

"If I remember correctly," said Xena, "there's no more jerky because someone ate it all this afternoon."

She smiled slightly, looking up at her young friend. Gabrielle opened her eyes wide, giving her best innocent look, her light eyes catching reflections from the crackling flames.

"There was hardly any left! And besides, I was hungry."

Xena set her sword aside and reached for her bedroll. "You're always hungry."

"I am not. I'm a growing girl, that's all, and I have to keep my strength up. Even you say so."

Xena nodded. "True. But if you keep eating all of our supplies, you'll break our horse's back."

"That's not—" Gabrielle started, but then grinned. Sometimes it was hard to tell whether Xena was kidding or not, she could keep such a straight face—obviously, this was a joke. Especially since Xena rode the horse most of the time. And there really *hadn't* been that much left . . .

Gabrielle turned back to the fire, hugging her knees to her chest. She never got tired of staring into the flames, watching the way they danced and shimmered against the darkness. Nearby, Argos was only a pale shape grazing quietly in the shadows of the trees.

It was really a nice spot that Xena had found for camping, a perfect resting place for weary travelers. The ground was flat and even, lightly covered with a scattering of clover and a few large stones. A tiny creek burbled nearby, just past a thick stand of pine trees. Compared to a lot of their camps, this was like a vacation . . .

Gabrielle yawned, the magical dance of the fire lulling her, making her sleepy in spite of her hunger. Having started out right after breakfast, they had ridden and walked all day to get to this comfortable spot. Xena liked to be on the move, even when there was nowhere in particular they had to be; she said that it was too easy to just stop and stay put, to let the days turn into weeks and then months of sitting still. No good if you wanted to get things done . . .

Xena looked up and then smiled fondly as she watched Gabrielle's head nod down to her knees then jerk up, only to droop again. Dozing in front of a fire, one of the simple but wonderful pleasures of life—one that Xena hadn't allowed herself in a long, long time. It was rare indeed that she felt she could let her guard down so completely, and trust that there was someone else to watch for trouble.

Xena sighed inwardly, then shrugged. No matter. In life, there were always trade-offs; true, she wouldn't feel comfortable sleeping soundly in front of a warming blaze, but there was pleasure to be found in watching over a good friend while she rested. It was nice that Gabrielle still had the faith of the innocent in these troubled times, even after all they'd been through together.

Xena decided to let her sleep a little longer and went about preparing their dinner herself, sharpening a stick to spit the rabbit she'd caught with her chakra; the metal hoop was quite handy for bringing down small game swiftly and efficiently.

That done, she tended to the horse and then laid out their things for bed, her sword always

4

within easy reach, her hearing trained for any unusual sounds in the forest or from the road. She wasn't well traveled in the western regions and the extra caution didn't cost her anything.

Gabrielle slept on, oblivious to the world around her—though, thought Xena wryly, if the scent of roasting meat didn't wake her, nothing would.

It was dark where Gabrielle was, dark and as silent as a tomb. She looked around, tried to get her bearings, but the blackness was so deep that she could see nothing. It was cold, too, and there was a strange scent in the air, like burning . . .

"Xena?" Her voice seemed to echo, a hollow, ringing sound, as if she were inside a huge room. "Xena!"

The only answer was her own voice, sounding strange and lonely as it echoed back at her.

She reached out with both arms, groping in the dark for a wall, a chair, *something*—but her fingers grasped only cold air and nothingness.

She started to feel the first gnawings of panic in her stomach. Where was she? Where was Xena? For that matter, where was *any-thing*—the fire, the camp, Argos?

And then, in the cool black silence, she heard something. A low, deep rumbling, a growling sound, soft and barely there at first—but it grew, rose up into a horrible roar that filled the air and pounded her senses.

A creature, a monster! It would have to be enormous, judging by the sound of it, and angry to the point of insanity, the pitch of its fury matched and surpassed only by her terror.

Gabrielle wanted to run, but she didn't know where the monster was, couldn't tell with the way it was echoing all around her. She needed a weapon, but she couldn't even find a *wall*, let alone anything to chase away a creature of this ferocity.

The smell of burning was stronger now, the roar of the animal closer. If only Xena were here! Gabrielle opened her mouth, screamed out her friend's name—

—but it emerged as a strangled whisper, the scream stuck in her throat.

Too late. The invisible thing had her, had laid its cold talons on her shoulder—strange, such a tiny claw, and it was shaking her now, and suddenly, instead of its mighty roar, it spoke her name in a firm tone of voice.

"Gabrielle."

All of a sudden, there was no monster, no coldness, no roar.

"Gabrielle!"

"Huh? What!"

Xena's concerned face hovered in front of her, the warrior's gentle hand on her shoulder, shaking her awake.

"You were having a nightmare. I thought you were going to roll yourself right into the fire, the way you were thrashing around."

Gabrielle shook herself, the last remnants of the dream fading away. She had fallen asleep, that was all; the burning smell had been wood smoke. And the creature . . .

"Oh, Xena! I had a horrible dream! It was so *real*, too, more like—like a vision!"

"Oh?"

"Yeah! I was all alone, inside this giant room—and there was a—there was this *thing*, but I couldn't see it, I could only hear it, and it was *huge*, as big as the world, and I couldn't get away—"

Xena frowned, but her eyes sparkled with amusement. "That's quite a vision. I guess that means we should avoid big rooms for a while . . ."

Gabrielle glared at her, but she wasn't really angry. Now that she'd said it out loud, it sounded less like a vision and more like a bad dream. Still, Xena didn't need to know that.

"I *do* have the gift of second sight," she mumbled, and then even quieter, "sometimes."

Xena grinned at her. "Of course. And sometimes, when you're hungry and tired and you fall asleep next to a hot fire, you have nightmares. But who can say? At least we can fix the hungry part—that is, unless your vision scared away your appetite."

Gabrielle's senses finally picked up the delicious scent of the cooked rabbit over the low flames, and she realized that Xena had already made dinner—for a change, it looked like something worth eating, too. Xena's cooking was usually pretty awful, unless you liked burnt stew and uncooked root mash.

Gabrielle's stomach suddenly let out a growl that almost rivaled the creature's screaming roar from her dream; she hoped that the flush of the fire hid the sudden redness she felt creeping up her neck. "Well . . . having visions really drains you, you know? I'm always hungry after one."

Xena nodded, all seriousness, but her eyes still sparkled. "We should eat, then. I wouldn't want you to lose your gift."

Gabrielle smiled and reached for her plate. "Exactly."

Just to make sure, she had several helpings.

Xena was already asleep, although Gabrielle knew that she'd awake at the slightest sound, so she lay on her bedroll quietly, careful not to make any noise. As always, she wondered how Xena did it—when *she* slept, it practically took a parade to wake her up; Xena, on the other hand, was up and fully alert if so much as a twig broke the wrong way.

She was tired, but she couldn't get the dream out of her head. It had to mean *something*. Perhaps not a literal creature—but she had a definite feeling that it had something to do with their future, and that it was something unpleasant. She sighed. An unsettling thought, to say the least.

It could have just been a nightmare. Gabrielle had made that mistake before, more than once. One time, she'd had a vision that a great eagle was going to swoop down out of the sky and carry off her family's milk cow, and *that* had seemed very real. Except that the cow had died of old age two years later, right in the barn.

But then, you never could tell with the gift of prophecy; it *could* have happened, but maybe she had changed the outcome somehow and saved the cow . . .

Still thinking of monsters and milk cows, Gabrielle finally slipped off into a deep and peaceful sleep.

Something in the woods.

Xena snapped awake, snatched up her sword, and stood, not questioning her instincts. Her sleeping ear had detected a sound that didn't belong; that was enough.

She crouched, ready, and waited. The fire had melted down to glowing embers, and the moon was low in the sky; it was late. After a moment, there was the unmistakable sound of footsteps through the woods, a clumsy crashing that let her relax a little bit; there were only two of them, whoever they were, and if they had trouble in mind, they probably would at least have tried to be quieter. Still, she stayed in a crouch; unexpected company in the middle of the night was not something to take lightly.

Gabrielle stirred and sat up, rubbing her eyes and looking around in confusion. Xena jerked her head at the sleepy girl, motioning her to hide behind one of the large stones near their beds. Gabrielle quickly crawled out of sight, making almost as much noise as their coming visitors; they would have to work on her stealth abilities.

For now, though—Xena raised her sword as the crashing came closer.

Out of the darkness, a young man stepped into the dim glow of the dying embers, his face dirty and tired. Right behind him was a much older man, dressed in the same simple clothes and wearing the same exhausted look. They had the air of villagers, peasant folk— and for a weapon, each carried only a staff. The younger of the two had a sling around his waist, probably for hunting—all in all, they looked about as threatening as a pair of wood-chucks.

Xena lowered her sword slightly. "Who are you?"

The two men turned at the sound of her voice, and their expressions changed dramat-ically, both at the same time, in a way that Xena did not expect at all, that caused her to lower her weapon even further.

Huge, unaffected smiles of joyous relief.

The older man spoke first. "Thank the Gods! We've found you!"

The younger man actually laughed out loud, a shaky sound of weary amazement. "Oh, she knew, she *knew*! Maybe there's still time!"

Xena frowned and stepped closer to the two men, curious now. "Time for what?"

Their smiles melted away, again as one, and the older man's voice became hoarse and frightened as he spoke again.

"Time to stop the end of the world," he whispered. "You are the only hope there is to stop it before it's too late."

2

Gabrielle poked her head up from behind the rock. "What?"

The older of the two looked surprised for only a second at the sight of Gabrielle, then nodded grimly. "It's true, and there's not much time left. She—she did say that there would be two of you, and she's been right so far. We should head back right away—"

Xena lowered her sword as Gabrielle stepped into view.

"Before we go anywhere," said Xena, "maybe you should explain. Sit down."

Both of the men nodded and stepped farther into the camp, finding places near the smoldering fire. Gabrielle reached for their morning stock of wood and set about rebuilding the blaze.

The older of the two spoke. "I am Zetes, and this is my son, Danaus. We're from a place not far from here—it's not a village, really, although there are almost a dozen families that live in the same area. Most of us are hunters, trappers—we grow our own food and take care of each other, just another group of woodfolk that live in the forests throughout the western hills."

The fresh wood on the fire slowly caught, the flames casting strange shadows around Zetes and his son.

"Two years ago," he continued, "an oracle came to live with us, Alesandra. Her powers are great—"

Danaus nodded excitedly and cut in. "She doesn't even use stones or sticks! She can see things in waking dreams, and this one time she foresaw that Ajax would break his leg and it happened the next day, and another time—"

"Danaus!" His father's voice was gruff and irritated.

Danaus flushed red and fell silent. "Sorry," he muttered.

Zetes fixed his son with a final scowl and went on. "Alesandra does have the gift, I assure you. And a month ago, she was carrying water from the river and suddenly fell down, overcome with a vision. She woke up and told us that she had learned a terrible thing, that the sun would die—"

Again, Danaus interrupted. "And that everything good in the world would turn to evil!"

Zetes glared at him, and again Danaus blushed.

Gabrielle felt a sudden surge of excitement. The vision she'd had—she *knew* it had meant something.

Xena bit at her lip and frowned. "And how am I supposed to stop this . . . prophecy?"

Zetes shrugged. "I'm not sure, exactly. But Alesandra said that there was one person, a woman, who could change the course of this fate. A warrior with raven hair and eyes like ice—"

"And—" started Danaus, but this time his father was too quick.

"*And* her traveling companion, also a woman, an innocent," said Zetes, nodding toward Gabrielle. "We're supposed to bring them—bring you, to Alesandra."

Gabrielle raised her eyebrows. "Hey, I'm not so innocent, you know. I've seen a lot of pretty rough business in my time, you'd be surprised."

She tried to sound tough and worldly, even

15

though Xena *still* hadn't trained her sufficiently in fighting skill; she knew a few things, certainly, but she didn't have even a tenth of Xena's prowess. Xena said that the loss of innocence wasn't worth the knowledge gained (Gabrielle didn't agree, but Xena was insistent on the point).

Yet, in spite of the slight embarrassment of being labeled naive, Gabrielle felt a warm, proud glow spark to life, deep inside. The oracle had mentioned *her*, specifically! *She* was going to help change the fate of the world . . .

Xena nodded slowly, thinking. "That sounds like us. But what is it, exactly, that we're supposed to do about it? Knowing the future doesn't mean you can change it."

Zetes sighed. "I know. But it's our only chance."

He looked down at the backs of his hands, dirty and scarred from a lifetime of hard work. When he looked up again, his dark eyes were filled with sorrow.

"I have children," he said softly, "and grandchildren. There's a whole world of parents and their babies." He paused, staring deep into Xena's eyes. "Life is hard, but it can be good, too. If you don't come with us, all will be lost."

Gabrielle jumped to her feet and reached

16

down to grab her bedding. "Of course we'll go with you, just lead the—"

"Gabrielle!"

Xena's tone of voice stopped her in her tracks. Gabrielle turned, suddenly worried; surely Xena wouldn't say no, not unless she thought they were lying. And yet Gabrielle's instincts told her that these were honest men—

Xena smiled at Gabrielle's fear. The young woman couldn't hide her feelings if her life depended on it. "Gabrielle," she said again, in a gentler tone, "these men need to rest. We'll leave first thing in the morning."

Gabrielle smiled, feeling vaguely embarrassed for allowing her thoughts to show so easily. Xena certainly teased her about it often enough—but traveling with such a woman as Xena wasn't easy, and one of the drawbacks was that Xena *always* seemed to know what was going on.

Zetes and Danaus both jumped to their feet, thanking Xena in voices shaky with gratitude. They decided to sleep just past the small creek so as to allow Xena and Gabrielle their privacy, but they gladly accepted Xena's invitation to meet again for breakfast before starting out.

As Gabrielle settled back down for the

night, she wondered how she would ever get back to sleep with so much going through her mind. Anticlimactic, to say the least, just falling back to sleep after such an event. Xena probably already *had*; the warrior could fall into her light sleep in the middle of a war zone, said it was one of the benefits of her past—being able to sleep when necessary, tired or not. Apparently monumental events or not, too . . .

She rolled onto her back and stared up into the sky, watching the stars glitter brightly against the early morning darkness. What would her own part be in this thing? What would Alesandra tell them? The sun dying? Was it a literal vision, or just one that symbolized something else?

When the morning dawned, they would be going to meet a real oracle, a woman who had seen *them* in her vision of the fate of the world. Most true prophets only saw little things, like if a baby to be born would be a boy or a girl, or if the crops would be good on a given season—and only then with the help of runes or notched sticks that they used as tools, to channel wisdom.

But an oracle who received waking visions—that was a gift indeed. And a power that Gabrielle wouldn't mind studying up on.

Her own tiny visions were often cloudy, and usually came in dreams. Maybe this Alesandra could give her some tips, just some general information to help her along . . .

With that happy thought in mind, Gabrielle snuggled into her bedding and closed her eyes, willing herself to sleep. Tomorrow was going to be a big day.

"So how did you find us? Did Alesandra tell you where we'd be?"

Xena addressed the question to Zetes, who walked alongside Argos while she rode. Gabrielle and Danaus had fallen behind, chatting happily away about something or other, as they had all through their light breakfast and the first leg of their journey. Perhaps Gabrielle had finally met her match in the talking department; Danaus was a nice boy, almost Gabrielle's age, but there seemed to be nothing he didn't have an opinion on. So far, he and Gabrielle had swapped stories on everything from horse riding to royal fashions.

It was just as well. Xena was curious about this prophet; she'd met many a charlatan in her day, greedy men and women who pretended to see the future in exchange for money. Zetes seemed like an honest man, and not one to be easily tricked—but wise men were fooled all of the time, or so it sometimes seemed.

Zetes nodded in response to her query. "At first, she wasn't sure, although she thought that you were heading west, toward us. Half of the menfolk in our part of the woods set out looking, me and Danaus included. When we couldn't find you, we went home and waited, hoping that she'd have another vision before it was too late—and yesterday, she said you were close, just to the east of our forest. Danaus and me, we left right away."

He smiled up at Xena, his lined, weatherbeaten face not so weary as it had been the night before. "I'm—We're all so grateful that you've decided to come and talk with Alesandra. It's rare to meet such a great warrior, who has the power to change the outcome of a prophecy."

"That remains to be seen," said Xena lightly, but she couldn't stop the pang of guilt that coursed through her at Zetes's kind words. Simple woodfolk like Zetes and his son—there had been a time when she had destroyed people like them without a second thought, taking what she wanted from their meager supplies and burning what she couldn't use. Killing those that stood in her way. A time that she could spend the rest of her life trying to make up for, and probably never succeed . . .

But that won't stop me from doing what I can, she thought firmly. *It's the least I can do.* If this prophet were the real thing and Xena could somehow stop the vision from coming true, it would go a long way toward making up for some of her own power-hungry past.

"I've heard of you, you know," said Zetes softly. "You have quite a reputation, even all the way out here; my wife has family in the east."

Xena arched her eyebrows. "And yet you came looking for me anyway?"

Zetes nodded and met Xena's gaze squarely. "Alesandra said that you aren't the same woman you used to be. And that blood no longer sheathed your sword, unless there was no other way."

Xena didn't show her surprise visibly, but the case for Alesandra being a true prophet was building. For a man like Zetes to seek her out in spite of her reputation—either this Alesandra was a very convincing liar or she knew of what she spoke. And it was true; Xena was as different now from her old self as night from day—

"We're almost there," said Zetes, interrupting her thoughts. "Just past that next stand of trees."

He motioned toward a thickly forested spot ahead, a small trail leading through the shade of the woods. Xena nodded and clicked her tongue against the roof of her mouth, urging Argos to go a little faster.

Alesandra awaited, and Xena was becoming quite interested in meeting her. At the very least, it would be a most unusual lunch.

They came to Zetes and Danaus's home as the sun reached its highest point in the sky, and both Xena and Gabrielle could see why they hadn't called it a real village. There were only a few houses, built of sticks and thick river mud, and not even a proper road leading to the dwellings.

Xena could see a few more tiny homes farther along the trail, gentle smoke rising from a few small fires between them. A middle-aged woman hung her washing from a tree branch nearby, a well-fed mongrel dog napping by her feet.

All in all, a pleasant enough scene. Xena could hear a river close by, and there was a small vegetable patch planted in a strip that ran next to a few of the homes.

"Mother!"

Danaus ran to the woman hanging up her wash and embraced her. A smile of pure joy beamed from her when she saw that Zetes and Danaus had been successful. She hurried over to greet them.

Gabrielle looked around, smiling at the children who peeked out from behind the doors of the tiny wood shacks. The small boys and girls wore expressions of awe and amazement, as if they'd never seen strangers—and it occurred to Gabrielle that they were probably in awe of them in *particular*, the two women that the prophet had named. Gabrielle tried to look cool about it, but she could feel her heart beat faster at the realization—of course they were amazed; *she* was supposed to save the world! Well, and Xena, too . . .

Zetes's wife nodded at them eagerly, nervously wiping her hands against her apron. "We're so glad to have you! Shandra, she's our best cook, she made a nice stew for lunch, and the men, they'll be back from workin' soon, too . . ."

She trailed off nervously, and glanced at her husband, who nodded at her.

"I guess you'd be wantin' to meet Alesandra, then," she said. "I'll go fetch her."

Xena dismounted, then walked Argos to a shady spot well away from the vegetable patch so he could graze. Zetes's wife had hurried off down the trail to one of the small houses, and Gabrielle had crouched down amid a group of grubby but delighted children.

Zetes and Danaus nodded to Xena, saying that they would go hurry the men's work so that they could eat soon. Xena stood by Argos, patting his neck gently, enjoying the cool shade and wondering at the way of life these people led. Simple but hard, surely—why would a prophet of Alesandra's power choose such a tiny place? If she was as incredible as Zetes and Danaus seemed to believe, why wouldn't she be in some great city, the oracle for a king? True prophets could demand any price they wanted for their services—

"*There* you are!"

Xena looked up to see Zetes's wife coming quickly down the trail, hurrying over to where Gabrielle stood with the group of children. Strange—why was she looking for Gabrielle? Xena walked over to join Gabrielle just as the older woman met up with them.

Zetes's wife reached out and took the hand of one of the children somewhat nervously, as if she were afraid to touch the little girl.

The child was perhaps twelve, a sweet-faced youth with butterscotch eyes and golden brown hair.

"Xena, Gabrielle," said the woman slowly, still barely touching the child's hand, "*this* is Alesandra."

3

Gabrielle's mouth actually dropped open as she realized that the great Alesandra was probably the same age as her little sister. Xena kept a straight face, merely cocking one eyebrow, but she couldn't help feeling a bit surprised; she thought she was ready for anything, but a pint-sized prophet?

Alesandra dropped a clumsy curtsy, bowing her head and then smiling up at the warrior princess. The smile was genuine, but Xena could see a kind of sadness in the child's eyes, a look she recognized. It was the same expression she'd seen in herself, long before—a child old beyond her young years, a gaze that had seen too much.

"Thank you for coming," said Alesandra, in a high, clear voice.

Gabrielle's mouth was still open. "Wait a minute—*you're* Alesandra? The oracle?"

Alesandra nodded, the smile fading, her gaze still fixed on Xena.

"I am. And we need to talk, right away. Please, come with me."

With that, Alesandra turned and started up the trail, past Zetes's wife and the other children, toward one of the small shacks. Xena noticed that the other youths shrank back slightly, as if afraid; even Zetes's wife quickly stepped out of Alesandra's way.

Xena shrugged at Gabrielle and then headed after the little girl.

Gabrielle caught up to her friend, eyes wide. "Is this a joke? I mean, she's a *child*, she can't be Alesandra!"

Xena shrugged again, still walking toward the tiny home where Alesandra must live. The little girl was just stepping through the small doorway.

"You think prophets are born old?"

"No, but—" Gabrielle struggled for the right words. "Well, I just thought she'd be a little more . . ."

"Old," finished Xena, smiling. "I'll admit, I'm a bit surprised myself. But I looked in her eyes, Gabrielle, and there's something about her that is greater than her years. We'll see what she has to say before we write this off as a joke."

Together, they stepped into the hut where the oracle waited.

Gabrielle was disappointed. Where was the bubbling cauldron? Where were the books of spells, the cobwebs and shadows, the musty, ancient *feel* that an oracle's lair was supposed to have?

Instead, there was a cramped but clean one-room house with a tiny window over the child's bed. There was a faded patchwork quilt folded at the foot of the wooden cot, and Alesandra had seated herself next to it, her little legs barely touching the dirt floor.

"Um. There's really not much room, but feel free to sit where you can." Alesandra seemed somehow even younger now that she was inside her home, dwarfed by even the tiny surroundings. Other than a small, splintery chair and the bed, there was no other furniture—and no decorations, except for a raggedy cloth doll seated on the windowsill. It was obvious that Alesandra lived alone.

Gabrielle sat on the edge of the cot, careful not to show her disappointment at the simple room. "Where are your parents?"

Alesandra sighed. "I don't know. They're

dead, I think—I grew up in Pottera, a fishing village up north. The people who raised me also had other children with no family—they were very kind to take us in. They told me that they'd found *me* asleep next to a piece of driftwood on the beach, with a note that just said my first name."

Xena had seated herself in the rickety wooden chair. "If these people are in Pottera, then why are you here?"

Alesandra dropped her gaze sadly to the floor. "I could always . . . see things, things that haven't happened yet, or that happened a long time ago; I thought that everybody could, I didn't know. But when I was able to understand enough to talk about it, I told Helena—she was the lady who raised all of us—and she got very upset and told her husband, Thoras. Then they told me I had to leave. They said that I was . . . bad."

Alesandra looked up, her eyes pleading. "But I'm *not* bad, I'm just different, that's all. Anyway, I was only nine or so, and I traveled for a week, I guess, staying near the sea so I wouldn't get lost—and I met a very nice man named Otus, who lived here, with the woodfolk. He had been traveling to buy supplies, and he brought me back to live with him."

Alesandra's eyes grew bright with tears as

she went on. "He was old, though, and he died last winter. The other people here take care of me, but Otus was like my father. He told me that I wasn't bad, that I was special, and he said that if he had a daughter, he'd want her to be just like me."

Gabrielle felt her own heart ache a little at the story. She reached out and took Alesandra's hand, squeezing it tightly. Alesandra smiled at her gratefully, blinking back her sadness.

"Anyway, that's how I came here. The woodfolk liked Otus, and they let me stay after he was gone. And sometimes I see things that can help them, like where there's a good place to hunt or when it's going to rain. I don't have any control over it, not really, it's like—" Alesandra shook her head. "It's hard to explain. I just *know* things sometimes. And I try to help, but every time I say something about what's going to happen, the people here get a little more nervous, like I'm *too* different. I think maybe they're scared of me."

Xena nodded slowly, remembering how the other children had carefully backed away from Alesandra; even Zetes's wife had seemed uncomfortable around her.

Alesandra sighed again, a heavy sound. "And ever since the day of the last full moon,

31

it's been worse. That's when I saw it."

"Your prophecy of darkness," said Xena quietly.

Alesandra nodded. "It's going to happen, Xena. I'd swear on it."

Gabrielle shuddered at the strong conviction in the little girl's voice. There was no doubting that *she* believed what she said; she sounded too sure to be making it up—and Gabrielle liked her, besides. Liked her, and could see that she was no liar. And if she wasn't lying . . . ?

Xena chose her words carefully, not wanting to seem disbelieving. "Are you sure that you had a vision? Maybe it was a bad dream . . . ?"

Alesandra stood and walked to Xena, holding out her small hands. Xena took them in her own, staring into the child's honeyed, searching eyes.

"I saw it as clearly as I see you now," she said. "And as clear as I saw you then. You are a warrior, fighting for good, but you weren't always. I saw a young girl crying when her brother was killed, and I saw that girl grow up learning to fight, to seek revenge for the wrongs done to her family. I saw her grow drunk on power, and then learn from her mistakes, turned away from her vicious self by a man stronger than any other man. And I saw her befriend a younger woman," Alesandra nodded toward Gabrielle, still seated on the bed, "an innocent girl who wanted adventure and excitement. I saw these two women traveling with a pale horse, and I saw that of all the people in the world, only this warrior woman could stop the horror that I saw in my vision—with a little help.

"That woman *is* you, isn't it? Now do you believe me?"

Xena stared back into Alesandra's eyes, shaken by the perfect truth of her words. There were very few in the world who knew so much about her, very few indeed. And there was no way that Alesandra could know so much of it unless . . .

"I believe you," said Xena quietly. "Now tell us the rest. And how we can stop it."

Alesandra smiled as if a huge weight had been lifted off her shoulders. Xena could see that the child had been afraid her tale wouldn't be believed.

"Thank you," she whispered, and leaned forward awkwardly to hug the surprised warrior.

Gabrielle realized that she was staring at the little girl hugging Xena, but she felt helpless to stop. Gods, this was *amazing*. Alesandra had just told Xena's whole life practically, reciting it like a poem or something! Gabrielle's disappointment with the child oracle had flown out the window; this kid was one powerful prophet, no question.

Alesandra sat back down next to Gabrielle, still smiling, but the smile quickly faded. "There are some things I didn't see," she said, "but I guess we can worry about that stuff later."

Alesandra closed her eyes, as if to remember more clearly. "It happens at a castle near someplace called Avernus, I know that much. There is a . . . man there, a young man, and I saw that he has no evil in his heart. He has a book, and with this book, he does . . . something, something wrong, a mistake. This mistake brings blackness and cold, but a horrible fire, too. I saw that the sun dies, and I saw all kinds of people who are smiling suddenly start to cry and be angry and shout. They raise weapons against each other, even against their own children."

Alesandra opened her eyes, and both Xena and Gabrielle could see the fear there. "The people I saw, their hearts all turned black, and I knew, in the vision, that they were everyone. I know it doesn't make sense, but I knew it, just like I knew your whole history, all at once—those people represented everyone in the world.

"Whatever this man does, it turns everyone bad, everywhere. And when that happens—when that happens, the world is over."

Gabrielle chewed at her lip, her heart pounding. What a terrible vision! She looked at Xena, read the cool confidence in her gaze, and relaxed, a little. This was serious bad, but if anyone could stop it, it was her friend.

Xena looked thoughtful. "What else?"

Alesandra slumped, all the life seeming to drain out of her voice. "Well, that's the part I don't know. I saw you at this castle, and I saw you with the book in your hands, before this man makes his mistake with it. When I saw that, that's when I knew all about you."

She looked at Xena hopefully, then at Gabrielle. "I saw all of that, but I didn't see *how*. I was sort of hoping that you might have some idea of what to do."

Gabrielle looked at Xena, who stared back, and then they both looked at Alesandra. The child's face was a picture of nervous fear.

"You *do* have an idea, right? Because whatever is going to happen, it's going to happen soon, sometime in the next month—there's not much time."

Gabrielle felt a stab of worry in the pit of her stomach, and she could tell from Xena's frown that she was feeling the same way. They were fresh out of ideas.

4

"Alesandra? Um, there's food ready, if your, uh, guests are hungry."

Xena looked up at the young blond woman standing nervously in the doorway, a tight smile on her face.

"Thank you, Shandra—Xena, Gabrielle, this is Shandra."

Both Xena and Gabrielle smiled and nodded, but Shandra was already turning away. Even Gabrielle noticed this time.

"I'm sure they really like you," she said to Alesandra. "They're probably just not used to having a prophet around, that's all. Some people just feel a little weird when they're around somebody who's different."

Alesandra smiled sadly. "I guess that's it. Thank you for saying so, anyway. Are you hungry?"

Gabrielle nodded, her stomach growling at the prospect of a meal cooked by somebody else. Xena nodded also, but Alesandra's story had taken away most of her appetite.

As Xena followed Gabrielle and Alesandra out of the room, she thought carefully about the child's terrifying vision. A castle near Avernus, she'd said. Neither of the younger women could know—they hadn't traveled as much as she had—but Avernus was a lake in the southern regions that most people avoided—for it was supposed to be near the entrance to Hades, the place that souls went after death. She'd heard many a tale about Hades and didn't credit much of what she'd heard as truth—but there were too many stories to discount them entirely.

She herself had never been to the Avernus region, but even the smallest of children had heard of Hades, usually as a warning—mothers used the stories to frighten their young into behaving. Hades wasn't necessarily a bad place, but the one constant in all of the tales was that the souls there were all eager to get out, to return to life. And the name was often howled in the heat of battle; "I'll see you in Hades" was quite a popular cry among the men she had once led . . .

Alesandra led them into the bright sunshine and toward a waiting group of men, women and children. The woodfolk were obviously waiting for them before starting the meal, and they watched Xena and Gabrielle with wary and respectful gazes as the two women received wooden bowls of steaming stew. After Alesandra got her serving, the others finally crowded around for theirs.

Alesandra led Xena and Gabrielle to a shady spot beneath a tree, where they sat down to eat. Xena noticed that the other woodfolk steered clear of the spot, even Zetes and his family. It was apparent that Alesandra intimidated them—they chose openly to sit in the harsh midday sun rather than join the child prophet.

Their loss, Xena thought, even smiling a bit as she began to eat. Afraid of a little girl they didn't understand. It was sad for Alesandra, but Xena had found throughout her travels that most simple folk rejected those who didn't fit in; they were too narrow-minded to accept that there were *good* differences as well as bad. And although Alesandra surely suffered now, it would be no great loss for her in the long run; prejudiced people weren't worth having as friends. The truth of it was a hard lesson to learn, but necessary.

Gabrielle eagerly dug into her stew and

exclaimed at the flavors: rabbit, fresh nuts and tomatoes—all seasoned with a skillful hand. She waved at Shandra, grinning.

"This is wonderful!"

Shandra cast the three of them another of her tight, nervous smiles and then went back to her own bowl.

Alesandra glanced up hesitantly at Xena as Gabrielle shrugged and continued eating. "Maybe when this is all over, you can drop me off in a city somewhere . . . ?"

Xena could hear the hope in the child's voice, and she smiled gently at the girl. Truly, Alesandra didn't belong here. Children needed more than just food and shelter, and an oracle could always find welcome in more populated areas, perhaps even some kind of training.

"I don't see why not. I thought that perhaps Gabrielle could stay here with you while I go to Avernus and see what the situation is. It shouldn't take more than a few weeks, and when I get back, we can talk about arrangements."

Gabrielle felt hot, angry blood rush to her cheeks as Xena spoke: Stay *here*? When they were a team? Over her dead body!

"Hey, I thought we would be in this together! You need me, Xena; you know that I could be a big help! Who's going to cook if I don't go? Or fetch wood, or take care of chores? Besides, I come in pretty handy sometimes, you know that . . ."

Gabrielle trailed off, noticing Xena's firm gaze. Time for a different approach. She fixed Xena with her most serious, world-weary look and tried again.

"I agree, Alesandra should stay here; the traveling would be too hard on her, and we don't even know what we're up against yet. We can come back for her afterwards. But I've *got* to go with you—I've got a feeling about this one, Xena."

Xena sighed. She knew her young friend would protest, and Gabrielle *had* shown that she was capable enough in a fight, in her own way—but this was just too dangerous. If this prophecy involved the powers of darkness, she'd have her hands full watching her *own* back; protecting Gabrielle on top of that would be too much.

"You'll both stay here. I've heard a few things about Avernus, and if the stories are true . . . It's settled, Gabrielle. I'm sorry."

As the two women locked stares, Alesandra set her bowl down and cleared her throat loudly. "Sorry to mess up your plans—but *all* of us have to go. The vision was clear; I saw all three of us at the castle. You're the key, Xena, and I'm not sure what Gabrielle and I have to do with it, exactly—but we have to be there. If you go alone, you won't be able to stop the prophecy."

Both Xena and Gabrielle turned to her, a slow grin stretching across Gabrielle's face, a frown across Xena's.

"See, didn't I tell you?" Gabrielle nodded excitedly. "I had a feeling about it!"

Xena gritted her teeth and spoke angrily. "And have you told us everything about your vision, Alesandra? Are you sure that's everything? You're not going to suddenly pipe up with some new, forgotten piece of information at the last minute?"

Alesandra chewed at her lower lip and dropped her gaze to the ground. "Well . . ."

Xena softened her tone. "Please, Alesandra. We have to know everything."

Alesandra wouldn't look up. "I saw the three of us go to the castle—but one of us doesn't come back. And I don't know which one."

They finished their lunches mostly in silence, Alesandra's final statement putting a damper on even Gabrielle's appetite. No matter how well prepared, food lost some of its appeal when there was a chance you wouldn't be around to enjoy it much longer.

Gabrielle glanced at Xena often, but the warrior was lost in thought, maybe thinking about what Alesandra had said—only two of them would come back.

Would it be Xena? Gabrielle watched her friend for a moment, wondering. No, she was too good a fighter, too skillful. There wasn't a man or woman alive who could take her in battle. Alesandra, then? She looked at the child, staring sadly into her half-empty bowl. It wouldn't be fair, she was so young . . .

Me, thought Gabrielle. *Maybe it's me who won't come back.*

The thought filled her with worry and a vague uneasiness. Maybe that dream she'd had about the creature, maybe that was a warning to her, telling her that *she* was the one who wouldn't return from this quest. It could have been the horrible creature of death, or something . . .

Gabrielle smiled slightly in spite of herself. The horrible creature of death! Xena would laugh herself silly if she heard *that.*

Finally, Xena looked up at both of them and smiled, and when Gabrielle saw that smile, most of her concern fell away. It was the same smile that Xena often wore into battle, a half grin that spoke of great confidence and certain victories to come; and more importantly, it was a look that meant Xena wasn't worried, not a bit.

"In my experience, outcomes can always be changed for the better," she said lightly, "especially when I'm around to change them."

Alesandra and Gabrielle both smiled back at Xena, and Gabrielle felt the rest of her fear evaporate; whatever they were up against, Xena could beat it—and as long as there was breath in her warrior body, she wouldn't let any harm come to either Gabrielle or Alesandra.

Xena gazed around at the warm, lovely day, watching the woodfolk gulp down their food, noting that someone had set a bowl of water down for Argos. It really was a nice place to visit, although she was glad that she didn't live here—already, her spirit cried out to move on, to begin the quest that would lead them to Avernus.

"Gabrielle, why don't you and I see what we can bargain for in the way of supplies while Alesandra packs her things? I'd like to start before the sun sets. We've got a lot of traveling to do, and apparently, not a lot of time."

Alesandra jumped to her feet and ran to get

started while Gabrielle cleared their dishes, her eyes fairly glowing with expectation. Xena was glad to see their excitement, but she couldn't help wondering what lay ahead of them. Although she was confident in her abilities, she knew that changing the outcome of a prophecy was not some kind of dare. She'd put on her best face so that Gabrielle and Alesandra wouldn't worry overmuch; the last thing she needed was to have two frightened companions to watch over. It was going to be hard enough having them along at all, but according to Alesandra, there was no other way.

She lay a hand against the hilt of her sword and stroked it absently; what the child had said, about a man with no evil in his heart, the man who was to bring about this horrible fate—what kind of man was this? And how could she stop him? She wouldn't kill a good man, or anyone who truly meant no harm; those days were behind her . . . but if there were no other way, and all the world depended on it? What then?

Xena sighed, and stood up. Wondering about it was pointless until she knew more; they would have to find this castle and meet this mystery figure, try to find out what motivated him. Perhaps then, she would know what to do.

5

The castle was old, the stones battered and worn by many years of harsh weather and life-times of secrets untold. In fact, it looked like a ruin, so desolate and hidden among the trees that the rare passing traveler wouldn't even notice it—and if they did happen to glance at the seeming rubble, they'd dismiss it as one of the many crumbling castles that littered the countryside. Especially here, near Avernus—most sane humans wouldn't dream of living here, and the few who had tried had left quickly. There were only a handful of people who even knew this castle existed, and fewer still who knew how strong and protected it truly was . . .

Telius sighed heavily. He would have to go back soon; there were things to do. It was just so lovely outside, so nice to be out in the sun, away from the cold stones that made up his life. In spite of the twisted, stunted trees and the ugly dried grasses, the air was fresh and warm, the skies mild and crystal blue. When he was a child, his father had often taken him for long walks outside the castle, sometimes all the way to Avernus, where they would sit and talk about things. There were no fish in the lake, no life at all, but it was still quite pretty, and it was there that Martus Bain had entertained his son with stories about kings and princesses and cities made of gold . . .

Telius sighed again, his heart heavy. It had been almost half a year since his father had passed on into the afterlife, but remembering those times still filled him with a deep sadness, remembering his father, Martus Bain, the great scholar and wizard; the man who had raised him with patience and love, and whom he had loved dearly in return.

Telius had few memories of his mother; she had died when he was only three from a strange sickness, what his father had called a seizure of the heart. It had been quick and painless for her, at least, but Telius knew that his father missed her greatly. He himself didn't remember her well enough to miss her, but he was often sorry for his father's quiet sadness.

He stood and stretched, then scattered the remains of his lunch on the ground for the ravens to eat. There were no other animals here, not so close to Avernus. The castle itself was protected by a powerful spell, cast by its builder long ago, so that the people and animals there could live undisturbed—but the grounds for several miles around couldn't sustain intelligent life. Apparently, the nearer to Hades, the worse it was—horrible and strange nightmares troubled those who slept there. The ravens, of course, were the exception, and Telius didn't mind feeding them on occasion.

"Lunch for you," he muttered, as he scattered the last of the bread crusts and fruit rinds among the gnarled tree trunks. He talked sometimes just to hear himself speak, fancying that he had a pleasant, deep voice. Truthfully, he was afraid he might forget *how* to speak if he didn't practice sometimes. He lived alone in the castle now except for Dunn, the family servant, and Dunn was a deaf-mute.

He started to walk the short distance back, feeling a weight gently settle on his shoulders the closer he got to home. He had lived in the castle all of his young life, nineteen years, and his father had lived there most of his—it was the only home Telius knew, and while he had always loved the place, it had just gotten too lonely since his father passed on. If there hadn't been so much to do, he might have considered moving away, going to a place with people and animals and *life*, maybe even a young, sweet woman who would want him as a husband . . .

Even as he considered these things, he knew it couldn't happen, not yet—maybe not ever. He had a mission, a great calling, and he couldn't abandon his home and his work.

Well, technically it was his father's work. His life's dream, really. Martus Bain had spent most of his long life studying, and had even learned a bit of sorcery along the way— and all to fight evil, to battle for the cause of good among men. The elder Bain had collected rooms full of books and spells, had devoted his time to learning all he could about the nature of evil so that he could war against it, perhaps even destroy it. It was why he had come to Avernus, to live at the very entrance to Hades. Where else? Hades was said to be the home of the Dark Gods as well as the souls of men—the eternal bringers of hatred and revenge.

But Martus Bain had been mortal, and all mortal men grow old and die. Telius's father had been a noble, good-hearted man and he had passed away in peace, confiding to his son that he would be happy to reunite with his long lost wife—but Telius missed him terribly. And so he would accomplish what his father had not, honoring his memory; he, Telius Bain, would destroy evil.

His father had *wanted* him to continue, he was sure of that. Fairly sure, anyway. On his deathbed, Martus had told him to try and be happy, to seek out whatever it was that inspired him—but he had also said to be very careful of all the books and scrolls in the castle, to make sure they were kept safe from the hands of the ignorant. Telius believed in his father's work, had even studied alongside him in later years, and he was sure that the warning was a kind of bestowal of fate, the handed-down gift of a lifework. What better way to keep all of that knowledge safe than to stay here and take over the studies himself? He didn't know half as much as Martus had, of course, but he wouldn't let his father's life dream go unfulfilled. He *couldn't*.

"I *won't*," he whispered harshly, as he reached the castle gate. It was a great burden, perhaps, to continue the lifework of a man as noble and learned as Martus Bain—but it was a burden he was proud to bear.

The gate was of heavy wood, lined with thickly wrought iron. Telius squatted down near the base and pressed one of the small stones set into the wall near the opening. The gate creaked open, and he tapped at three more of the tiny rocks, careful to touch them in the right order. The whole castle was rigged with keystones and other mechanisms, all designed to keep intruders out; without the proper combinations, it would be very hard indeed to get inside unscathed.

Telius slipped through the heavy gate and closed it behind him, his skin already prickling with the drop in temperature. No matter how warm it was outside, the castle remained cool and chill, even in the open courtyard. He walked across the small dirt yard, stopping briefly to check on the penned animals; it was Dunn's job, but Telius had always liked dealing with the livestock. Pigs, a few cattle, a coop of chickens—along with the vegetable garden around the other side of the woodshed, they ate quite well.

Telius considered looking for Dunn, but decided against it. The servant kept to himself, spending most of his spare time weaving on a small loom in one of the guest rooms or silently playing with Nox, his shaggy black dog. Besides, Telius wanted to study. He'd found a spell in one of his father's oldest books that looked promising.

He stepped into the main hall of the castle, stopping briefly to gaze up at the solemn portrait of his father as a younger man; the picture dominated the entranceway. Telius had inherited Martus's looks, which he was thankful for—a strong, square jaw, straight nose, dark hair and eyes—handsome, he supposed. Not that it mattered much, here . . . But it felt good to have taken after his father in looks as well as ambition. Telius liked feeling connected to Martus, and he was reminded of the strong physical bond each time he passed the portrait.

Telius turned down the long, winding corridor, walking through the soft and cold shadows that gathered low against each crumbling stone wall. Although the castle seemed small from the outside, it had been built to deceive; many of its passages tilted downward, ending in rooms that lay underground. This added to the outside appearance of a ruin; piles of broken stones lay atop a network of halls and rooms, but those passing wouldn't know it. The chilled air smelled faintly of earth, mixed with lingering scents of incense and wax, and the chambers Telius passed were empty and darkly silent.

Finally, after more twists and turns and two sets of stairs, he arrived at the room where his father had spent much of his time, a room that Telius now practically lived in. He stepped through the stone doorway and went to a dark wooden desk set to one side. The room was empty except for the desk, a chair and several stacks of dusty books, some piled almost chest high. Across from where he sat down, a bare stone wall spanned the length of the room; the wall was deeply etched with strange symbols and words written in long dead languages. Telius could read most of it, and knew the darker rocks to be runes of protection and other kinds of barrier stones; it was a wall that could be opened, although it never had been, not since before his father's time.

As a child, he had been afraid to visit this room alone; he had imagined that if he were very quiet, he could hear voices through the thick stones of that wall, shouts and cries, screams of misery and anguish. It was no secret that some souls could not rest in Hades, particularly those of evil men and women— they longed to be back among the living, as did the souls of saints. Redeeming themselves, he supposed. He'd pictured fires made out of shadows on the other side, and a heavy, foul stench like burning hair. Perhaps an aura of vain hope, woven through it all, an atmospheric overlay of dreams dead or dying, reaching out to take him in . . .

He knew better now; nothing came through the wall or went through it, not without the proper rituals. But he *did* know, as his father had, something that maybe no one else alive knew—that the Castle Bain, in spite of its decrepit appearance and modest means, was the only guard against what lay on the other side of the wall. There were other entrances to Hades, of course, but the wall of this very room was the only one that mortal man had any control over.

Which meant that Telius Bain was now its master—and someday, perhaps soon, he would find a way to make his father proud.

Telius flipped open a book and started to read.

6

The shadows were already growing longer, the heat of the afternoon at its worst as Xena cinched up Argos's saddle. Alesandra had given her a pitifully small sack of clothes to pack, only a few dresses and undergarments—and the tattered rag doll that had sat on her windowsill. Apparently Otus had made it for her, her only remembrance of the man.

The woodfolk had all gathered around to watch them leave, and as Xena swung the child up onto the saddle, Zetes stepped forward slowly.

"You're a good girl, Alesandra," he said quietly, and most of the others nodded along with him. "I know that Otus would be proud of you, and I hope that wherever you go, you find happiness."

He smiled awkwardly and then nodded at Xena. "Gods be with you," he said, and then stepped back.

Xena climbed up behind Alesandra and reached around for the reins, clucking her tongue at the horse. Gabrielle was still chatting away at Danaus, probably trying to get her fill of talk before their journey.

"Gabrielle," she called, and the young woman tore herself away from the animated Danaus to join them, her cheeks flushed.

"Sorry," Gabrielle muttered. Xena thought she talked too much sometimes, but it wasn't often that she met up with people her own age. Not to mention *cute* people her own age . . .

Danaus smiled shyly at her, raising his hand to bid them farewell. Gabrielle waved in return, and Xena turned Argos back up the trail that had brought them here.

There were several cries of "Good luck" and "Safe journey" from the gathered assembly, although no one seemed particularly sad to see them go. Alesandra cast one look at the people over her shoulder and then turned to face the trail ahead, obviously glad to be going.

"Are you going to miss them?" Xena asked quietly.

Alesandra shrugged. "Zetes was nice to me, I guess. But no, not really—I didn't belong there, somehow."

Xena nodded. "I know what that's like. When this is all over, we'll find somewhere for you to belong."

Alesandra grinned up at her, and Xena smiled back warmly. For all her power, Alesandra was still just a child; and assuming they all survived this prophecy, Xena would make sure that she found a home.

They backtracked to another offshoot of the trail and then found a rutted road that veered to the south; the path wasn't in very good condition, but Argos was a smooth mount and at least they weren't having to hack a path through the woods. The air was sweet with early summer smells, and the afternoon heat was slowly fading, dropping along with the molten sun as the afternoon prepared for evening.

Xena kept Argos in a slow walk, as the road was lined with berry bushes and Gabrielle wanted to gather enough for supper. Judging from the blue stains around her mouth, she was eating as many as she was collecting.

"Here," she said brightly, giving Alesandra a handful of the dark but slightly sour berries.

Though it was still too early in the season for them to be properly ripe, Alesandra accepted them with a smile.

Gabrielle was curious about the child, but wasn't sure what it was, exactly, that she wanted to ask—or how to ask it, for that matter. Alesandra obviously hadn't had many people eager to talk to her about the gift of second sight, and she might feel uncomfortable discussing it.

On the other hand, perhaps she needed to talk to someone about it—especially someone who had also experienced visions of the future. Well, *almost* visions; Gabrielle hadn't ever had one that came true *exactly* as she'd seen it, but many events had involved similar elements . . .

And besides wanting to help the child, she *liked* Alesandra, and was glad for more company—Xena could be so silent at times; traveling with others was a good time to practice her own social skill . . .

After walking alongside Argos for a few minutes, Gabrielle finally blurted out, "You know, I've had some pretty strong visions myself."

Alesandra's eyes widened. "Really? You have the gift of prophecy?"

Gabrielle shrugged. "I don't know if I'd say

'gift' exactly, but I've had a few dreams that were very real, you know? And right after those dreams, something always happened."

Alesandra nodded excitedly. "Yes, it's like that for me, too! You just *know*, right?"

Gabrielle frowned. "Um—yeah. I mean, no . . . know?"

Alesandra nodded again. "It's kind of hard to explain—mostly, when I see the things I see, it's not like a play that happens in front of me. I mean, I don't *see* people running around and doing things. It's more like . . . like a memory or something. It's like how you know the sun rises, or that water comes from a lake or river. I just suddenly have this information in my head, and sometimes I see faces or things, but mostly it's just this knowledge. I just know."

Gabrielle bit at her lip, still frowning. "Really? For me, it's more just like a regular old dream at night, except I have these strong feelings about things when I wake up. Like I'll feel that something good is going to happen, like that."

"When was the last time you had such a dream?" Alesandra asked.

"Oh, just last night! I dreamed about— Oh, I must have dreamed about the castle!" Gabrielle looked to Xena, her eyes wide. Xena's face was hard to read as usual, but she seemed interested in the conversation.

"Yeah, that must have been it! I dreamed that I was alone in a dark, stone room and there was a giant creature in there with me! It was terrifying, and I woke up thinking that we should be very careful, that something bad was waiting for us. Isn't that right?"

Xena nodded thoughtfully. "Maybe it *was* a bit of prophecy." Then she smiled teasingly at Gabrielle. "There's a first time for everything, I suppose."

Gabrielle scowled up at her but decided not to say anything; in truth, a lot of her dreams hadn't turned out to be particularly visionary. Still, Xena didn't have to be so *smug* about it.

Alesandra frowned. "Well, I didn't see any . . . unusual creatures in my vision. Are you sure that's what it was?"

Gabrielle shook her head. "I *thought* so, but I couldn't see it. It definitely sounded like one."

Alesandra thought about it for a moment and then nodded. "In the vision, I did sense a nonhuman presence, something that will play a part in the prophecy—but it was just a dog. The true creature, perhaps you saw it through your dream . . ."

Xena glanced down at the child in front of

her, suddenly very curious. "What do you remember about this . . . dog?"

Alesandra craned her neck around to look at Xena. "Not much. It was big, but not bigger than a cow, I don't think; it was like . . . a dog, but not a dog. The funny thing is, I thought there was something wrong with it, like it was deformed—like it had more than one face, somehow. But that's silly, isn't it? Anyway, that's all I remember."

Xena tightened her grip on Argos's reins but was careful not to show her emotions. Was there any way . . . ?

"Alesandra," she asked calmly, "how many faces would you say it had, if you had to choose a number?"

The child shrugged. "Three, I think. That's why I thought I was wrong about— Xena, is everything all right?"

Xena had pulled the reins, bringing Argos to a stop. She dismounted, then reached up to help Alesandra off of the stilled horse.

"Here is as good a place as any to stop for the night," she said, and offered both of her younger companions a smile. She looked around and saw that there was a decent grassy spot just off the road—and the growth of the low shrubs nearby meant that there was a pond close at hand. It actually *was* a good resting place, although that wasn't why she had stopped . . .

"Xena?" Gabrielle seemed worried by the sudden decision to halt.

Xena sighed. "Let's get a fire going, and I'll see what I can find for supper. And then I'll tell you what I know about Avernus."

Xena smiled at them both again, but she couldn't help the slight gnawing of apprehension in her gut at what Alesandra had said—for the child had just described Cerebrus, the three-headed dog that was supposed to guard the gates of Hades. And according to the legends, the ferocious creature was almost impossible to kill.

"When you first mentioned Avernus, I knew what we would probably be up against," said Xena, "but I didn't want to jump to conclusions."

They sat around the snapping fire, Gabrielle and Alesandra across from her, their dirtied dinner bowls stacked against a weathered tree stump. It was dark, only the barest glimmer of moon overhead, and the crackling flames did little to drive the night away from their camp. The shadows were deep, flickering limbs of blackness that seemed to play over every shape, changing and molding the rocks and trees into animate things.

Gabrielle shivered in spite of the fire's warmth, hugging her knees to her chest as Xena continued, the warrior's strong features softened by the dancing light.

"I have heard many things about Avernus, many wild stories that probably hold as much truth as a murderer's heart. I don't believe much of what I hear, since most people love to spin tall tales, adding details as they go along. But most rumors start with a grain of truth, however small—and the one thing that all of the stories agree on is that Avernus is a lake that stands on or near the entrance to Hades."

Gabrielle's mouth dropped open, and she felt her heart begin to hammer loudly in her chest. "Hades? Xena, you think Alesandra saw—"

"Cerebrus," Xena finished, and nodded. "Yes. The three-headed dog that is said to guard the gates of Hades. I've heard that there are many gates, and I've also heard that there are only a few—but the one at Avernus has been whispered about more often than any other. As I said, I didn't want to make any assumptions, just because Alesandra said Avernus—but the creature you described this afternoon, Alesandra . . . Cerebrus keeps the lost souls trapped in Hades from getting out, and intruders from getting in. Or so the stories say."

Gabrielle's mind was spinning. She had heard stories, too, about the dark world that was supposed to exist beneath the ground, but somehow hadn't made the connection to Cerebrus earlier. As a child, she and her friends would make up tales about Hades to scare one another, whispering about winged monsters with red eyes and sharp teeth that snuck out to kidnap little kids—

"But I thought those were just *stories*," she said out loud.

Xena shook her head slowly. "I'm sure many are. I've heard a thousand names for Hades and for the gods that are said to rule there—Pluto, Dis, Orcus, the Furies. Even Tantalus, the evil king who starved many of his people. Who can say which are true? I'm not prepared to give any of them credit . . . Hades is supposed to be where *all* souls go after death, good and bad."

Xena paused, suddenly deep in memory. "I knew a man once, long ago, who claimed to have visited Avernus. He had been a mercenary, someone who is paid to fight—Nisus was his name, and he was one of the bravest men I've ever known. He was the type of man who laughed in the face of death, and bowed down to no one in battle. And yet after his journey to Avernus, he hung up his sword and became a holy man, saying that he hoped never to travel there again—and if it meant leading the life of a poor saint, he'd gladly give up his livelihood. He said that he'd suffered the most horrible nightmares while sleeping by the lake's shore, visions of eternal suffering by loss of hope, souls crying out to redeem themselves—''

Alesandra, who had been still and silent, spoke softly. ''Did this man actually go into Hades?'' Her voice trembled with fear and her brown eyes were wide, almost panicked.

Xena suddenly realized that she had said too much. She shook her head, trying to find some reassurance for the frightened girl. She thought it was important for them to know what she did, but she hadn't meant to scare Alesandra with her musings. For all of her power, Alesandra was still a child. ''No. Nor did he find the entrance. I guess we'll just have to stay awake while we're there, won't we?''

Xena grinned now, darting a meaningful glance at Gabrielle. Gabrielle took the hint, realizing that such frightening stories were too much for Alesandra. Especially after dark, with the shadows dancing, transforming the trees into strange creatures . . .

Gods, I'm scaring myself! Gabrielle shook off her nerves and also smiled at Alesandra.

"Pretty scary stuff, huh? Good thing we don't have to get to sleep right away; we can talk about it more tomorrow, if we want. In the meanwhile, look what *I've* got."

Gabrielle reached into her bag and pulled out a small sack of berries that she'd saved from earlier. Alesandra smiled slightly and reached for them.

"Have you ever heard the story of the beautiful princess Mallory and the time she found a golden locket that turned out to be enchanted?"

Alesandra shook her head, her eyes wide again, this time with curiosity. If she knew she was being shamelessly distracted, she hid it well. Gabrielle started to tell the tale, glad to have such an eager audience. Besides, it had been her own favorite story when she was younger. And it had a happy ending, that had nothing to do with Hades or three-headed monsters or nightmares . . .

Xena stared thoughtfully into the fire, pleased that Gabrielle had changed the child's focus—but Xena was still roaming the rooms of her past, remembering. The man who had ventured to Avernus, Nisus—she had fought alongside him, even respected him; not a man she would have chosen to face in battle, if given a choice. She had often found herself searching battlefields for his face, even in the midst of fighting—and she had been deeply shaken by the change in him when he'd returned from his journey, more shaken than she cared to admit. There had been a fear in his eyes that had never been there before, a shadow in his gaze that had almost frightened her with its sincerity. He had become a totally different man, and he hadn't even *seen* the gate to Hades, let alone gone inside.

Xena watched the flames crackle, and was glad that she hadn't told any of the other stories she had heard; Alesandra had been scared enough without knowing any more, especially the more believable accounts of Hades.

Because the one part of the story that never changed, no matter who told it, was that those who stepped inside the gate were never seen again. There *had* been myths spun of mortal souls gaining the living world again, but Xena thought that those stories were parables rather than truthful account.

No one left Hades; it was the one truth that Xena could believe, without doubt.

7

Xena woke up at the first chilled touch of dawn, the air still heavy with the fading darkness. Her sleep, as usual, had been light but dreamless; although she had never thought to analyze it overmuch, it was as if her bloodied past were her only real nightmare, a horror far more potent than any dark dream . . .

She rolled out of her bedding and glancing over at the two sleeping girls, reached for the wood that Gabrielle had set aside for the morning fire. Gabrielle, as always, was a picture of innocent peace, her face open and untroubled in rest, her tousled blond hair falling gently across her brow. Alesandra also looked innocent, although her child's face seemed somehow taut, her skin too pale, as if she worried even while she slept.

How strange it would be, to have such a powerful gift—and for one so young, the burden must be heavy. Xena could relate to feeling different, but fighting better than most men wasn't cause for the kind of ostracism that Alesandra had suffered, and would suffer. There were many who cursed the name of Xena, and with good cause—but it was a hatred for deeds done. Alesandra was feared and cast out simply for being herself, for using her visions to promote change.

It wasn't always easy for Xena to keep a positive view of her fellow man, as there was much ignorance in the world and often innocents suffered for it—but if she had completely lacked hope, there would have been no point in her trying to change anything. She knew that the essence of her life now was the effort to keep the scales of good and evil more fairly balanced, for everyone. She could hope for no better, as most people clutched their ignorance to themselves, their narrow-mindedness a kind of shield. But helping others to see their potential—to help someone like Alesandra learn that she was strong, and that the ignorance of others could be overcome—this was a way for Xena to promote change for the better without even lifting her sword . . .

She smiled to herself, stacked the kindling into a pyramid shape, and reached for her flint. In the early mornings, her mind liked to try and get at the meanings of life. She knew she wasn't a philosopher; she wasn't witless either, but she believed that it was all a game in a way. There were those better suited to deep philosophical thought than she ... more patient than she would ever be in the confines of the human mind. There was a part of her that strove to conquer injustice in a more physical way, and she could not deny it. The great scholars perhaps did not possess her drive to keep moving, to use action sometimes instead of words.

Enough with the depth, and on to the first battle of the day ...

Trying to get Gabrielle to wake up without having to dump cold water on her—a combat experience almost every morning. She started the fire, feeling strangely peaceful with the task, then turned to where Gabrielle slept.

"Gabrielle," she whispered, then repeated, louder, "Gabrielle."

Gabrielle rolled her head to one side and mumbled in her sleep. She said something that sounded a lot like "oofmasna-gluh." Bright and alert, as always.

Xena crept closer, grinning. "Hey," she said

softly, "I've made you a nice breakfast. It's all ready."

"Mmm?" Gabrielle was half-awake now, a dreamy, hopeful smile on her lips.

"Yes," said Xena. "We're having toasted grubs with cold, heavily congealed root jelly. Think of those little creatures, wriggling through the cold jelly—"

Gabrielle sat up, rubbing at her eyes. "Wha— Are you serious? That's . . . that's *disgusting*."

"Well, then, since you're awake, why don't *you* tend to breakfast?" Xena smiled prettily.

Gabrielle scowled at her, stretching her arms over her head and yawning at the same time. "Gee, what a good idea," she said, heavy on the sarcasm. Toasted grubs? With Xena's cooking, one could never be too sure; Gabrielle would be *delighted* to make something—anything, as long as she got to cook it.

At the sound of their voices, Alesandra opened her eyes and sat up groggily. "Hi."

Xena smiled at her. "Good morning. Did you sleep well?"

Alesandra nodded, smiling back wearily. She turned to Gabrielle, who rummaged through their food pack. "Can I do anything to help?"

Gabrielle shook her head. "Not unless you

can lay eggs. It looks like dried pork and brown nuts, unless Xena wants to go hunting."

She turned to her warrior friend, frowning. "We didn't get much from the woodfolk. Do you know if there are any villages farther south?"

Xena shrugged. "I can't imagine why there wouldn't be, although we have enough dried goods to last over a week, even without my hunting. I'm sure we'll find somewhere to restock before we run very low."

Alesandra had already started to roll up her bedding. "Yes, there is a place—I can't remember the name, but Otus used to trade things there for metals and cloth, things the woodfolk couldn't make. He never took me with him, but I'm pretty sure it's only a week away, maybe less."

"Great," said Xena, nodding. Although the hunting was plentiful now, they would need to have more dried goods for later; stories had it that the land near Avernus was a barren place, the woods there desolate and lifeless.

There was no need to tell her companions that; last night's conversation had made Xena realize that although Alesandra might be a prophet of high order, she was still young enough to accept legends and half-truths with an open heart—at least at night. They would reach Avernus in only a couple of weeks and find out what it was really like; worrying about it beforehand would not change anything.

Besides, Xena knew that, in spite of herself, she would worry enough for all of them.

The next few days were uneventful, falling into a simple pattern: sleep, travel, break for lunch and then go on until the sun dropped low in the sky. The weather was good, the rains of late spring already past, the air filled with the breath of blossoming new life. Their supplies were running low, but Xena noted that the road they traveled on was improving—a sure sign that they were nearing a populated area.

Gabrielle and Alesandra struck up quite a friendship as they traveled, the younger girl obviously looking up to Gabrielle as a real woman of the world. Gabrielle was happy in the role and enjoyed reciting tales of her and Xena's quests and journeys, along with her own wealth of heroic adventure stories.

Alesandra was thrilled by the attention, and Xena was glad to see that Gabrielle had broken through the girl's initial shyness about herself. Although, thought Xena grimly, if she had to hear the story of Prometheus one more time, she was going to have to stuff her ears with moss; it was Alesandra's favorite, and she begged to hear the tale of the fire-giver as often as Gabrielle would tell it. Coaxing Gabrielle to speak was no hard task, either . . .

By late afternoon on the sixth day after leaving the woodfolk, they had reached the outskirts of the village. At first, there were only a few scraggly gardens to signify the community's nearness, the weedy patches rich with the smell of manure and guarded stiffly by poorly dressed scarecrows.

As they got closer, they started to pass small, ramshackle huts where dirty children stopped their outdoor games to gaze up at their passing with wide, silent eyes. Gabrielle smiled and waved at some of them, but the children were obviously unaccustomed to seeing strangers; most ran inside or just stood there, as if struck dumb by the sight of other human beings.

Xena was used to such a response, particularly from adults. The sight of her armor and weapons usually drew wary looks from the small-town people she encountered—not to mention that there were no other women warriors traveling the land, at least not that she'd heard lately. Xena's reputation as a bloodthirsty fighter often preceded her. Opinions took longer to change than it had taken her to change her ways, she knew; her name was tainted by a long and warlike past. She could only hope that someday the name Xena could be spoken without fear or disgust . . .

The first true community building that they passed was a temple of some sort, although Xena couldn't tell who it was devoted to. Xena had never chosen an allegiance to any god or goddess herself, but then she'd always found it hard to put too much faith in something for which there was no tangible proof. She had never been able to decide if that was a fault or an attribute . . .

When they passed a second, and then a third, shrine, still without reaching the heart of the town, Xena started to feel a bit uneasy. The most populated of cities were overrun with temples, true—but from the looks of things, this was not a thriving community. As far as she knew, there weren't any cities in this region big enough to support so many temples.

"Alesandra, are you sure you don't remember the name of this . . . village?"

The child, still riding in front of her, shook her head and then craned her neck around to look at Xena. "Actually, maybe I do—it's . . . um . . . Osterus? Or Oserus, or something like that."

Familiar sounding . . . "Osetus?"

Alesandra smiled, nodding. "Yes, that's it!"

Xena felt even more uneasy, although she wasn't sure why. She could see the buildings of the town now, coming into view—a stable, more houses, and yet another temple. Not much of a village, really, as small and dusty as many she'd passed through. A widening in the road and a scattering of shabby wood or stone structures . . . What was it? She'd heard of Osetus, something about it, but she couldn't quite place the story. Gabrielle had stopped to pick a few daisies growing alongside the road, and hadn't heard their conversation; Xena called back to her.

"Gabrielle, have you ever heard of Osetus?"

She hurried to catch up, smiling, and reached up to tuck one of the small flowers into Alesandra's hair. "Osetus? It seems like—yeah, that's in one of my stories! It's that town in the south somewhere, where everyone is very religious—all the people there are into some kind of nature worship, and they're strictly anti-magic—prophecy, fortune-telling, all of it. I'm pretty sure that's the

79

place where they used to burn witches; you know, 'Anyone who casts spells is unnatural,' that kind of thing. Why?''

Xena brought Argos to a sharp stop, but too late; they were on the main road of the town, and at least a dozen people had stopped in the street, watching them with distrustful eyes.

They had reached Osetus, and if the people here found out who Alesandra was, they'd try to kill all three of them.

8

He'd found it.

It was amazing, unbelievable, seemingly *impossible*—that in only six months of searching, Telius had discovered what his father had spent his whole life looking for. Not just a spell, but *the* spell, the incantation that could conceivably end the threat of evil forever.

Telius was in his room, pacing, too excited even to sit down. His mind was buzzing with the possibilities—a new hope for all the people in the world, a new foundation to build upon; redemption for lost souls, all striving to amend their evils. If it worked, and he saw no reason why it shouldn't, the oppressed souls of the dead would be released from Hades, free to work toward a better way . . .

He stopped walking and grinned to himself, realizing that he was thinking too far ahead. Once again, his gaze was drawn to the desk at the foot of his bed where the book lay open, its pages yellowed with age.

Open to the page that would change the fate of humanity.

He sat down on the wooden stool in front of the book, searching for the phrase that had first alerted him to the importance of the spell.

Ah, there it was! He spoke the words aloud, marveling over the sound of them. "If these things be done at moon's full light, the Path be opened—and at that Path be a Creature most Foul, that keeps the tortured from Peace. That Beast will be undone with the last of the Words, leaving Freedom for all Souls beyond . . ."

Telius couldn't seem to stop grinning. He read the words again, silently, probably for the fiftieth time in the last hour. It was so simple—the "Path" was surely the entrance to Hades, which was said to be a long, shadowy hall. And the "Creature" was almost certainly Cerebrus, the guardian of the entrance, a three-headed dog that kept the souls inside; he'd always heard from Father that Cerebrus probably couldn't be killed, but here it was, a spell so simple that a child could complete it.

To kill the oppressor of souls! The Bain name would be written and sung about for generations to come—Telius Bain, the savior of mankind! If only his father were here to claim his rightful share of glory, to see the miracle that he had worked so hard to achieve . . .

His grin faded a bit. Truly, Martus Bain was the name that should be remembered; without him, none of this would be possible. Telius wouldn't have known anything about spells or magic if his father hadn't taught him—and just because it was he who had finally found the right incantation, that didn't make his father's search any less important.

Telius frowned, wondering how his father could have missed this book. He had found it at the bottom of a huge stack in one of the spare bedrooms; it hadn't been hidden or anything. The name on the dusty tome had caught his eye: *A History of Nether*, a title that meant it obviously had something to do with the Underworld . . .

On the other hand, there were so many books and scrolls in the castle that no one man could possibly read them all, even in ten lifetimes; perhaps his father had simply never gotten around to the books in that room.

Martus Bain had been a collector of all kinds of books, and had accumulated hundreds of them by himself—but there had been thousands already here when he moved in, an unheard of number for a single collection. Few kings kept more than a few hundred.

The history of the castle was somewhat mysterious; no one knew exactly when it had been built, or how long it had been unoccupied before the Bains moved in. Martus had often tried to ferret out its origins, but had never had much luck—all they ever knew as fact was that a great sorcerer by the name of Trajen had lived here more than two centuries before, and that many of the books had been his. Martus had thought that it was Trajen who cast the spell over the castle, to keep the inhabitants safe and free from nightmares. Trajen *may* have been the builder, too, or at least the architect of the strange traps and mechanisms that kept unwelcome intruders from sneaking in. The many complex and built-in devices certainly *seemed* magical, although there was no way to be sure—but whoever had created them, or the castle itself, Martus had always marveled at the incredible efficiency and had taught his son to appreciate the complex design . . .

Telius sighed, wishing once again that his

father were here. It didn't seem right, Father dying just months before this book was found! There had been so many hopes through the years, so many promises that had turned out to be falsely made—spells and rituals that had seemed like answers but had failed. Martus had tried scores of magical rites to try and stem the flow of evil in the world, and all to no avail. And now, here it was—as obvious as words on a page, and Martus Bain wasn't there to read them. It didn't seem fair.

Ah, but life is not fair! Telius heard the words in his head that his father had so often spoken, usually with a gentle smile. *To expect fairness from life is like expecting water from stone!*

Telius smiled himself, and felt his spirits lift as he looked down at the spell again. Life *wasn't* fair, but sometimes it was just—Martus was gone, but his legacy had carried on, and had come to fruition through his only son.

The ritual really *was* amazingly easy. The caster of the spell was supposed to light nine candles in a circle around himself, then draw another, smaller circle inside of it, directly in front of the hidden gateway. There he would stand and recite some magical words in a variety of different languages, and the gate would become visible.

Telius didn't quite understand that part. If the gate was behind the wall, how could it suddenly be seen? He figured that it was some kind of dissolving spell. Magic was a strange practice, indeed.

Cerebrus would be at this visible entrance, and all Telius had to do was say three words to "undo" the creature. He scanned the list until he found them—"Sacritil, Zeniphous, Amithese." He didn't recognize the language, but then, he had a long way to go before he'd be as learned as his father was; Martus probably would have known where they were from . . .

Telius stood and walked to the small window set into the wall, squinting out into the courtyard against the afternoon light. The moon would not be up for hours yet, but he believed that it was still less than half-full. If only it were later in its course! He didn't know how he would rest or eat or even *think* properly, knowing that he held the key to the future—and that he couldn't use it for another fortnight.

Again, his father's voice in his mind, a lesson that had always been a hard one for Telius to learn: *Patience, my son, patience. All things come to pass, in their own time.*

Telius sighed, and sat down on the edge of his bed, staring at the length of the shadows cast in the yard outside—as if looking hard enough might make them grow faster. If wishes were dreams, beggars would ride . . .

Eventually, he lay back and closed his eyes, exhausted from the adrenaline that had coursed through his veins since he'd found the book early that morning. And in spite of his certainty that sleep wouldn't come, he faded into a deep and peaceful rest, where dreams of glory and praise embraced him with warm and loving arms; and where his father stood beside him, smiling proudly at the son who had brought peace to the world.

9

Before any of the townspeople of Osetus drew near, Xena leaned closer to Alesandra and whispered in her ear.

"Don't say anything, just follow my lead."

She sat back up in the saddle and darted a bright smile at Gabrielle as one of the men broke away from the others and approached them.

"It would appear that we're in Osetus, Gabrielle! How fortunate to happen upon such a pleasant village while traveling to find Alesandra's kinfolk, don't you think?" *Please, take the hint* . . .

Gabrielle looked confused for only a split second before she smiled back. "Yes, it *is* fortunate! I've heard stories about the kindness of the people here; in fact, I once met a woman who lived in Osetus for a while, I can't remember her name but I think—"

"Gabrielle, we should introduce ourselves," Xena cut in smoothly. Gabrielle had a tendency to talk a situation to death; all they needed now was for her to make up something that could be proved a lie—then they'd *really* be up a creek.

The middle-aged man who stopped in front of them had the stern, unsmiling face of someone with little or no sense of humor, dressed in the simple white robes of a cleric or some other holy official. Before Xena could say anything, the man spoke to Gabrielle.

"You knew someone who lived here?" His voice was rough and gravelly.

Gabrielle had the good grace to shoot a quick, embarrassed glance at Xena; obviously, she realized her mistake. She then smiled at the man and rolled her eyes self-consciously.

"Oh, me and my memory! I was thinking of—*Oesitrus*, that's a town over on the coast. But this is *Osetus*, right?"

The cleric nodded slowly, somewhat suspiciously, then turned his gaze to Xena and Alesandra and spoke harshly. "I see your sword, woman. What business do you have here?"

Xena kept the smile on her face but bristled inwardly, almost wishing that she were still the old Xena—her previous self would have taught this piggish man a thing or two about manners . . .

"My name is Xena, and I'm traveling with my companion, Gabrielle, and our ward, Alesandra. This child is an orphan, and we are journeying south to search for her relatives. We had heard that she might have an uncle this way . . ."

The man frowned. "Where is this uncle supposed to be?"

Xena gritted her teeth, hard. "I'm sorry, I didn't catch your name . . . ?"

He frowned at her for another long second, then nodded slightly, his brow easing. "Excuse my manners. I am Saji, one of the three town leaders of Osetus and First Father of the Worshipers to Ling, the God of Truthful Pith—as was my father before me." Saji seemed to swell with pride at the sound of his own title; Xena could actually hear him capitalize the letters.

Pith! What's pith! Xena tilted her head to one side quizzically, realizing that making a joke right now could be dangerous—*too bad*.

"I'm afraid I don't know of Ling," she said, keeping her tone respectful. Saji had the slightly strained and self-righteous look of a religious fanatic, and poking fun at such a man would be a mistake—particularly if this town was full of men like him. Xena was glad that he hadn't recognized her name, at least— a closed-off religious community like this probably didn't know much of the outside world.

He seemed to relax a bit more, on familiar territory now, and his manner became patronizing and more than a little insulting. "Pith is the essence, the core of all that is life. Ling is the god of this core, the beginning and end to all that we see. He is the god of everything that man can touch with his hands, a denial of the evil that comes from flights of spirit—for the spirit that leaves the body is forever tainted. The body, like the land, must never go untended."

As Saji spoke, several of the townspeople behind him nodded, some of them even touching their own faces—some kind of religious gesture, Xena supposed, smiling nicely as if she understood the rhetoric of Ling. She tried to steer him elsewhere, without seeming disrespectful. "Well, as I said— we're looking for kin to this girl, and we know only that this uncle lives in the south, if he lives at all. Perhaps he's here? His name is—" Xena grasped quickly for a name, "Vanid; he's an oat farmer."

Saji shook his head. "No, there's no one in Osetus by that name. And only those who worship Ling are welcome to settle here."

He looked at Xena's sword again, and at her chakra. "We *don't* welcome trouble—but if you're just passing through, I won't take away your weapons . . ."

Xena smiled and nodded, thinking that if he even tried, she'd give him a headache he wouldn't soon forget.

"I must ask, though," he continued, "are you or your companions believers in the evils of sorcery or trained in the visions of foul prophecy that by nature denies the goodness of Ling?"

Gabrielle had been watching this exchange closely, and kept a smile on her face as she shook her head along with Alesandra, following Xena's lead. Xena was glad that Gabrielle had learned to keep a straight face in dire situations. Lying wasn't a favorite hobby of Gabrielle's, but there was more at stake here than just her honesty; Alesandra would not be able to defend herself.

Xena handled him easily, acting mildly surprised. "No, we're not trained in anything like that. We would just like to buy a few supplies and then move on—if that's all right with you."

Saji nodded. "Fine. You can find some dried goods and some fabric for sale at the shop of Trilo, over there." He pointed to a small, dirty building next to a stable. "And if you're seeking merchandise, the widow Leus makes leather cups and bowls and sells them out of the second temple—you would have passed it on the road in. The ironsmith works out of the stables."

He bowed stiffly at the three of them, his lined face still solemn, almost angry. "Again, forgive my manners. We don't get many visitors here."

"Gee, I wonder why," whispered Gabrielle, as soon as he was well out of hearing distance. "He's so charming."

The other townsfolk seemed to lose interest as Saji left; they wandered away to wherever it was they had been headed before.

Xena dismounted and Gabrielle helped Alesandra off of Argos. The girl was nervous, her light brown eyes flashing with anxiety.

"What if they find out?" Alesandra whispered. "What did he mean? I'm not foul or evil!"

Xena glanced around quickly. "Quietly, okay? No, of course you're not. The people here are practicing a religion that says prophecy is bad, that's all—they don't know any better." She smiled gently. "You have nothing to worry about; we'll just buy a few things and be out of here before you know it."

Alesandra nodded, but her gaze was still uneasy. "I guess I know now why Otus never brought me along," she whispered. "All he ever told me was that I wouldn't like it."

Gabrielle took Alesandra's hand. "Well, he was right, wasn't he?"

Alesandra nodded, and the three of them surveyed the town silently. There was an oppressive feel to the place, as if nobody laughed much, or sang. Even the staring children that passed by, pulled along by their stern mothers, didn't seem to be as active and happy as children were supposed to be.

"Let's get this over with," said Xena, and they walked toward the shop that Saji had pointed out for dried goods, leading Argos along. She looked around for someplace to tie him, but there were no hitching posts to be seen.

She sighed. "Gabrielle, why don't you and Alesandra stay here with Argos? I'll be quick."

Gabrielle nodded, taking the reins. She looked around at the lengthening shadows, the afternoon sun still bright yet somehow desolate against the dusty road. "Hurry, okay?"

Xena nodded and stepped toward the open-air shop, ducking beneath the low wooden overhang. It wasn't ten paces from where Gabrielle and Alesandra waited, which made her feel better about leaving them; Osetus was a bit too strange for comfort.

Xena had traveled through religious villages before, and for the most part, they had been peaceful places. The men and women who chose that life were generally just looking for a safe and loving environment in which to raise their families, and weren't especially quick to judge others. Osetus, on the other hand, seemed like the kind of town where harsh judgment was not only accepted but encouraged.

A short, darkly bearded man, presumably Trilo, stepped out of a back room to greet her. He looked her up and down with the same suspicious gaze that Saji had, and spoke gruffly.

"What do you want?"

Xena looked over the stocked shelves that lined the back wall, nodding to herself. Not a bad selection for so small a town; the God of Pith must be very proud. "Two rounds of

bread . . . a haunch of that dried meat . . ."
She saw several bags of dried apples and
smiled inwardly. Gabrielle would tear into
those like there was no tomorrow. "And
three of those sacks of apples."

She reached into her money pouch for a few
pieces of silver while Trilo tied her purchases
together, and then she glanced out of the
shop; a young woman and her small daughter
were approaching Gabrielle and Alesandra,
smiling hesitantly. The little girl was reaching up to pet Argos, her eyes wide and shining.

In spite of the pleasant scene, Xena suddenly felt anxious; they had to leave—she felt
it in her gut, and she never questioned her
instincts. She dropped a few coins on the
counter and scooped up the parcel, hurrying
outside to join them.

The young mother had reached out to pat
Alesandra on the head, and Alesandra was
taking the woman's hand in her own, smiling—

—and then a strange expression flitted
across Alesandra's face. Xena saw a light
come into those honey-colored eyes, and
somehow Alesandra suddenly seemed older,
wiser—

"You're with child," Alesandra said softly,

her voice deeper and more mature than her normal, light tone. She spoke as if in some kind of trance, as if taken over by a spirit older than her own, yet still her own, it seemed. An older Alesandra, perhaps, returning to speak through her younger self.

"A son, and he will have his father's dark eyes. He won't be an ironsmith like your husband, but will take to the land, growing crops. He'll be healthy and strong, but will break his arm when he's a child, climbing a tree. Don't fear, it will heal well. He will be creative, too, as your own mother was—"

Xena rushed forward and pulled Alesandra away from the woman, grinning easily. "Alesandra, are you making up stories again? Please excuse her, she has quite an imagination—"

It was too late. The young woman had picked up her daughter and was backing away from them, a look of terror on her plain face. Alesandra shook herself, looking around confusedly, and then stepped toward the woman and child.

"Wait, please! I'm not bad, that's not bad—"

The woman held up her daughter like a shield and started to babble, softly at first but rising quickly to a shout.

"Witch, a witch—how could she know? I

haven't told *him* yet; nobody knows that I am with child! No one! A witch, the child is a witch! *The child is a witch!"*

Gabrielle grabbed the packages from Xena and shielded Alesandra as the warrior pulled her sword—and the townspeople of Osetus poured out into the street, angry and shouting.

10

They were surrounded. As the woman with the little girl continued to scream, the townsfolk all gathered around Xena, Gabrielle, and the frightened Alesandra, and shouted in confused, panicky voices.

Xena spun, looking for an exit, but there was no way to get them out of danger without hacking a path through the unarmed crowd. She saw no glints of steel, no flash of arrow; these were simpler folk, not fighters—angry but not necessarily dangerous, at least not yet. She wouldn't want to injure any of these fumbling zealots, which would surely happen if it came down to fighting—

But they will not harm any of us, either.

Xena resettled the heft of her sword, her grip loose and ready.

"What is this? Quiet, all of you! *Quiet!*"

The shouts died down as Saji cried out for silence, stalking into the circle of people. He turned toward the young woman and her daughter.

"Tura, what happened?"

Tura stammered out a reply, watching Alesandra with fearful eyes. "The child touched me—and foretold!"

A hush fell over the mob as they found a focus for their anger, their eyes turning toward Alesandra. She stared miserably at the ground, her slender jaw quivering.

"What did she say?" Saji spoke softly, but his voice was full of cold menace.

Tura clutched at her daughter, still obviously afraid. A burly man wearing the leather apron of an ironsmith stepped out of the crowd and put his arm around her, encouraging her to speak.

"She—she said that I was with child!" Tura whispered raggedly, her tone suggesting that Alesandra had told her to expect leprosy soon.

Saji seemed to mull this over for a moment, biting at his lip as he did so. He finally looked up at the giant man who held Tura. "Barus?"

The ironsmith, Barus apparently, looked at his wife in turn.

Tura nodded at him. "I believe it true, husband. I did not plan to tell you until I knew for sure." Fresh tears welled up in the woman's eyes, and her voice shook and strained as she grew almost hysterical in manner.

"The witch said that he would have your eyes, and would take to the land . . . Barus, what are we to do? I had so wanted a son with you, and now this—Barus, it is *evil*!"

At her final words, the crowd seemed to move closer, muttering prayers and curses alike in harsh and blackly malicious tones. Argos whinnied nervously, and Xena raised her sword high; if it came to hacking their way out, so it would be—

Saji held up a hand, stilling the mob. He turned to Xena, his expression grim. "Is this true?"

Xena didn't waver, keeping her sword raised. "No. She is not a witch, and she's not evil."

Saji didn't seem concerned by the shining weapon. "But she foretold the birth of a son by Tura?"

"Yes. And I would think that Barus and Tura would be happy, knowing that they're to be blessed with a healthy child. There are many who would feel gratitude, or—"

"Blasphemy," someone in the crowd

whispered. Several others nodded, their eyes cold.

Saji glowered angrily. "You lied to me. You said that none of you were trained in this evil!"

Xena shook her head. "I told the truth. The girl *is* untrained; her prophecy is a gift from birth."

"We don't welcome such 'gifts' here! The god Ling does not suffer such . . . such *insult*!" Saji's voice was that of a preacher now, his gravelly tone rising in self-righteous fury as he addressed the mob. "The child has forever cursed the lives of Barus and Tura with her foul prophecy! Don't you *see*, my people, that we are all infected now? That we live and die together, work together—are *cursed* together, by the misfortunes to even *one* of us?"

The group of villagers muttered and murmured louder in dark agreement. Xena moved closer to Gabrielle and Alesandra, ready to defend first, always defense first.

Gabrielle hugged Alesandra tighter, looking around at the villagers. "Well, hey, we can see that we're not welcome," she said, a bit too brightly. "We'll just get out of your town, you know, hit the dusty trail and leave you guys alone."

Saji ignored her and spoke directly to Alesandra, who was still somehow holding back her tears. "By the Declarations of Ling, you have tainted the happiness and prosperity of the ironsmith Barus and his family with your evil. Because of you, Ling may choose to disown them, as punishment. That so, Barus, ironsmith and husband to Tura of Osetus, now has the right to decide *your* punishment."

Xena lowered her sword slightly, but stayed alert to sudden movement. "No. I am responsible for bringing her here, and I will take whatever punishment is to be given."

Alesandra looked up at her fearfully. "No! It's my fault. I didn't mean to say anything, but when she touched me, it was such good news, I thought she'd be happy—I thought that maybe she could see that it's not bad, *I'm* not bad!"

Xena kept her cool gaze on Saji's. "I take responsibility. Agreed?"

Saji looked to Barus, who glanced at his sobbing wife and then nodded, his huge face angry and flushed, dark eyes flashing. Saji turned back to Xena.

"Agreed."

Barus stepped toward them, slowly clenching and unclenching his giant, calloused fists, the muscles in his arms flexing with power. He was easily a half head taller than Xena, and probably outweighed her by four stone.

"Throw down your weapons," he growled, pulling off his apron as he walked closer, tossing it to the ground. "I'm going to kill you with my bare hands. If you survive, which you won't, then maybe you can leave with your soulless skins—but if you die, we'll burn all three of you, and your *companions* will not have the luxury of death first."

He was close enough now for Xena to see the foamy spittle in the corners of his mouth, to see the glazed hatred in his eyes. To *smell* his fury, a horrible, sour sweat.

"We'll burn you like the witches you are!"

Without a word, Xena handed her sword to Gabrielle, holding her free hand palm out, toward Barus. The townspeople fell back, eyes bright with religious mania, caught up in the hungry spirit of a small but fanatical mob. The giant ironsmith stopped and waited, his powerful hands fisted.

Xena gave her chakra to Gabrielle, who looked worried. "He's *huge*," she whispered, taking the hoop. "If you need me—"

Xena shook her head, gaze still fixed on the ironsmith. "Their town, their rules, one on one. Just watch out for Alesandra; I'm going to be busy."

Xena lowered her hand and then circled slowly away from him, and away from Gabrielle and Alesandra. She could see by the way he moved that he wasn't trained to fight. His steps were wide and clumsy, his center was off-balance—but he was also strong, much stronger than she; if he caught her, he could crush her easily, breaking her neck as if it were a twig.

With a roar, Barus rushed forward, arms outstretched. Xena jumped to one side, spinning around with a side-kick that caught him in the ribs.

Barus grunted, even angrier now, and snatched at her arm. He grabbed her wrist and jerked, pulling her off-balance.

Xena went with the motion, realizing that he meant to break her arm. As he put pressure on her wrist, she half-crouched, allowing her arm to bend. The motion brought her close to him, enough for her to be spattered by his rank sweat.

She dropped lower, and used the flat of her free hand to strike at his neck, a blow that would have felled most men—but Barus seemed to be made from the iron he forged. He dropped her arm but stayed standing, face red with fury. She danced backward lightly.

He bent over and rushed her again, bellowing, head down. Too fast—he would be on her in a second—

Xena leapt forward, knees up, her high, trilling cry echoing through the street. As Barus passed under her, she somersaulted across his back and turned, landing behind him. Her leg shot out, foot arched back, and struck behind his knee, hard.

Barus stumbled and fell, landing on the dusty ground with a strangled cry. He jumped to his feet, his lower lip bloody now from the impact. He wiped at it with the back of one meaty hand, then spit—a tooth spattered to the dirt. He grinned at Xena, a sick smile of blood lust, and then ran at her again.

Enough of this, thought Xena, waiting until he was right in front of her before she moved. Just a small step to the left. He was too intent on his run to see her stick out her foot.

He tripped and fell, this time harder than before. He was slower getting to his feet now, and Xena could see that he wouldn't last much longer. He relied too much on his strength, his pure power, and she was outmaneuvering him easily.

She could hear the surprised cries of the townsfolk as Barus circled her again, his steps faltering and unsure now. Obviously they had expected him to beat her. She smiled a little to herself, wondering if they would apologize for their hostility before seeing the three of them out of town . . .

Barus had lost his grin, but not his anger. He spit again, the foamy substance bright red. Keeping his eyes on Xena, he looked for an opening.

"You can't win," she said gently. "There's no shame in it—just stop; you can stop this. We'll leave, and you can—"

He roared and hurled himself toward her, his fists raised—

—as Xena jumped and spun, a flying kick aimed at his head. Barus ran right into it, the heel of her foot catching the top of his skull with incredible force.

He stopped short, opened his mouth as if to speak—and his eyes rolled back, showing white. He dropped like a sack of manure, his unconscious form hitting the ground in a cloud of dust.

"Barus!" Tura broke away from the crowd and ran forward, to kneel beside her fallen husband. "You *killed* him!"

Xena looked at her calmly. "He's not dead, although when he wakes up, he might wish he was. The punishment is over."

She turned to Saji, who looked as if he'd just swallowed a live fish—his face was red and sweaty, his eyes bulging. He started to speak, but all that came out was a strangled *gah* sound. The townspeople stood silently, apparently not knowing what to do. Gabrielle grinned at Xena from where she still stood with Alesandra, the child watching Xena with an expression of amazement.

"Saji, we will leave now, as spoken by Barus. He said that if I survived, we could go."

He didn't say anything, and she decided to take his silence as agreement. She turned toward Argos, glad that no one had died, no real harm had been done except for a broken tooth and a sore head—

Behind her, Saji broke the stillness with a scream of rage.

"Kill them! Get the witch, the women, grab them and kill them! Ling will not be appeased until they are *dead*!"

Xena was running before he'd finished, running for Gabrielle and Alesandra, but they were already being pulled away from one another by the shouting crowd. The men and women of Osetus were grabbing for sticks and stones, ready to do Saji's bidding.

With a raging scream of her own, Xena leapt unarmed into the crazed mob.

11

Gabrielle struggled against the powerful arms that held her, then bit down on a hand that brushed across her face. A man shouted, and she was released. Xena's weapons had fallen to the ground, but there were too many people, too many legs and feet kicking up the dust—

—and then Xena was there, spinning and jumping, dropping the villagers one at a time. A woman holding a big stick was disarmed by a well-placed slap; the man who had grabbed Alesandra was felled by a blow to the knee.

"Gabrielle! Help Alesandra!"

Gabrielle ran to the scared child, lashing out at a snarling young farmer who tried to stop her. It was a lucky punch, hitting him hard on the chin; he stumbled back, and

Gabrielle grabbed Alesandra and pulled her away from the crowd.

Argos pranced anxiously in the midst of the shouting townsfolk, and Xena trilled again, a high call that would tell the horse to hold still. Argos obeyed instantly.

There were still fifteen or twenty of them standing, many carrying makeshift weapons—sticks, rocks, the handles of hoes and other farming tools. One elderly man held a wicked-looking scythe, the curving blade flashing maliciously in the late sun.

Xena leapt into the air, slapping her hands down across Argos's back, vaulting up and over him. She kept her legs splayed, striking two of the villagers in the chest, one with each foot. Ribs snapped. They fell, and stayed down. She landed, spun—

—and saw that four of the armed townspeople were headed to where Gabrielle and Alesandra stood, a hundred paces away. She only had a few seconds before they reached them.

Xena caught a glimpse of her chakra, the metal glinting against the dust by her feet. In one swift movement, she caught the shining hoop up and launched it, the kick sending it high into the air.

The man with the scythe rushed forward at

the same moment, and Xena ducked the blade, turning and driving her elbow into his stomach. The man let out an *oof* as the wind was knocked out of him and he dropped the weapon—

—as Xena caught the chakra, the metal landing easily in her hand. She vaulted back over Argos, this time landing squarely in the saddle. With the slightest of pressure from her boots, the horse lunged forward, headed for where Gabrielle was, the young woman sheltering Alesandra with her body. The armed foursome were raising their weapons to strike.

Xena trilled out again, used her trained instincts to mark the villagers in a split second—and the chakra flew, glittering, to knock four weapons out of four hands, bouncing between them almost faster than the eye could see. The attackers yelped and backed away in confusion; Gabrielle snatched up one of the fallen clubs, readying herself in case more came.

Xena deftly spun Argos around to face the mob—and saw that it wasn't much of a mob anymore. Those who hadn't been knocked down or injured didn't seem to know what to do now, confronted with an opponent they couldn't stop, let alone understand. Many had dropped their weapons; others were crouching down near their fallen neighbors, their expressions openly confused. A few had gathered around Saji, perhaps looking for direction.

Xena got down off of Argos, watching the villagers warily. Gabrielle and Alesandra joined her, Gabrielle handing her the chakra before silently taking the horse's reins.

Xena walked slowly toward the leader of Osetus, noting that none of the townspeople had been seriously injured, or at least not as far as she could tell; they had gotten off easy. She was no longer the cruel and careless woman who would have laughed to see them in pain; she had chosen a higher path—a way that didn't call for the murder of innocents, a way that seemed to contrast sharply with their own.

Xena met Saji's angry gaze full on. "Is this what your god demands?" she asked softly, then raised her voice so that the rest could hear: "Do you worship a god that would demand the life of a child?"

She looked around at the villagers and found that none would meet her gaze. Except for Saji, whom she faced again.

"We— The God Ling denies prophecy," he stammered, his eyes less angry and more uncertain. "He is the Creator of all, and will not stand for . . . He won't stand for . . ."

Saji trailed off, looking around at his people, his children. They watched and waited.

Xena arched her brow. "Ling created everything? He is the maker of all?"

Saji nodded, his face seeming older than it had before, more haggard.

She turned and addressed all of them, her deep voice carrying easily across the crowd. "Why would Ling create a child who is evil? Alesandra did not choose her vision; does that mean that Ling did *not* create her?"

She looked at Saji. "Or does it mean that perhaps it was Ling who gave her the gift of sight in the first place? That it is her natural self, to foresee?"

Saji didn't answer, but Xena could see in his eyes that she had made a point, however small. He wasn't stupid or crazy, she could see that—simply ignorant, so certain in his religious zeal that he hadn't questioned anything for a long, long time.

"Barus and Tura are going to have a son," continued Xena. "A son with his father's eyes. You should rejoice for them, rejoice in this blessing from your god. That Alesandra saw this thing—perhaps you should think about how she knew at all; if your god is the

115

Creator, perhaps she heard it from Him."

Saji still made no reply, and Xena could see that he wasn't going to change his ways overnight, or the ways of his people. But she could also see the thoughtful way with which he looked over at Alesandra, that question still in his eyes. Not a lot, but it was something.

Xena turned to Gabrielle and Alesandra. "Let's go," she said, and when she lifted Alesandra onto Argos's back, none of the townsfolk moved to stop her. She scooped up her sword, sheathing it quickly, and then led the horse past the staring villagers.

As they passed Barus, who was sitting up groggily with Tura's help, she saw the woman place a hand across her lower belly and smile hesitantly at her husband.

Xena imagined that once the young woman had held her healthy infant boy, she might not be so quick to judge in the years to come.

Within minutes, they were back in the woods, the package of dried goods tied securely to Argos's saddle, the town of Osetus behind them as the sun began its slow descent into the western sky.

Gabrielle let out a pent-up breath. "I never thought I'd be so glad to leave a place! Those people were nuts!"

Xena shrugged, still walking alongside Gabrielle. "Not nuts. Faithful to the point of blindness—they believe what they believe because they believe it, no questions." She smiled a little, thinking of the look she'd seen in Saji's eyes.

"But people can change," she added softly, almost to herself.

Alesandra was upset, her face a picture of misery. From her seat on Argos, she stared sadly at the ground, holding back tears. "I'm sorry, Xena, Gabrielle. If it hadn't been for what I did—"

"—they might never have learned to see," finished Xena. "It's all right. I have a feeling that the people of Osetus might be changing their tune before long."

She smiled up at a surprised Alesandra. "You may have just altered an entire religion. Because of what you did, those people are going to be forced to reevaluate the way that they think. And maybe the next prophet who wanders through will be welcomed instead of shunned."

Alesandra's eyes shone brightly. "Really?"

"Really." Xena grinned at Gabrielle. "Although I think maybe we'll go *around* Osetus on the way back, hmm? Give them some time to work out the details?"

Gabrielle nodded wholeheartedly, shuddering at the thought of revisiting the town. They walked along silently for a few minutes, each lost in her own thoughts, then turned a corner on the wooded path. The moon came into view, already up, still barely visible in the early evening light.

"Almost half-full," said Gabrielle, trying to make conversation. "You know, the Goddess Aphrodite once said . . ."

Gabrielle trailed off when she saw the look on Alesandra's face. The girl had fixed her gaze on the ghostly moon, and her skin had gone milk-white.

"Alesandra?" Xena pulled on Argos's reins, bringing him to a stop. "What is it?"

Alesandra spoke softly, but her voice had the same tone as before, when she had seen the future child of Tura and Barus. "How soon?" she whispered, her voice both young and old at once. "How soon before Avernus?"

Xena realized that Alesandra was "seeing," and she answered quickly, her tone gentle. "Perhaps two weeks."

"Then we must hurry," said the child, not blinking, staring at the half-moon, entranced. "When She is full, he will act. When She is full, our time is done, the Words spoken. He does not see, will not heed his father's words, he will undo the Beast—"

Alesandra faltered, then shook herself suddenly, looking to Xena, just a child once more. It was as if she had lost the train of the vision, slipping back into herself. Her eyes were wide and frightened by whatever she had seen.

"The moon! When it's full, whatever he's going to do, that's when he'll do it!"

Xena frowned. "You said that he would undo the beast, Alesandra—who will? Did you see him? Was the beast Cerebrus?"

Alesandra, tired from the full day of ups and downs and tired of being visited by prophecy, suddenly burst into tears.

"I don't know! All I know is that we have to get there before the moon is full or it's going to happen!"

Gabrielle rushed to comfort the girl, calming her with soothing words as Xena gazed up at the moon. Two weeks before it rose full and round, and it would take them that long to get to Avernus—not counting the time it would take even to *find* this man. And he might not want to be found . . .

Xena sighed, wishing that someone else had been named in this prophecy of doom. Two weeks?

It was going to be close.

12

The night of the full moon was only a week away, and Telius could hardly wait. The candles were already in place, the proper words memorized, and if there had been a spell that would make time speed up, Telius would have jumped at the chance—unfortunately, there was no such ritual. Or at least none that he knew of.

Telius had sent Dunn into town for supplies—not that they needed any, but Katil, the nearest town to Avernus, was easily a week away. Telius didn't want the spell to be interrupted, even by chance, so he'd told Dunn that he was in desperate need of ink, that his supply had run short. By the time Dunn got back, the rite would be a week past and the world would be at peace . . .

He felt a little guilty about lying to Dunn, who had always been a faithful servant and seemed like a nice enough man—but if the spell *didn't* work, Telius didn't want anyone to know of his failure.

"It *will* work," he whispered, then looked up at his father's image. "I know it, I can feel it!"

He was standing in the entryway to the castle, having just returned from another solitary picnic outside. The portrait of Martus Bain seemed to look down approvingly from its place in the main hall, his father blessing him with his kind demeanor, his dark eyes smiling at Telius.

Telius sat down wearily on the stone floor, still gazing up at the image of his father. He hadn't slept well the night before, only a few hours; as the fateful day drew closer, he found it harder and harder to relax. It was calm and peaceful here, the entry stones warm from the afternoon sun shining in. His belly was full from the sandwiches he'd had for lunch.

If only pictures could talk, he thought sleepily, *then I could tell him all about it; and he would laugh and talk with me, the way we used to . . .*

He closed his eyes, just a quick rest, and he

could hear the crows outside, their harsh cries seeming far away.

"Telius," said his father. "My son."

Telius looked up and around, his eyes wide. *Could it be—* "Father?"

There was no one in the hall, no one who could have spoken. Telius turned his head, and a flicker of movement caught his eye, from the wall above him. The portrait of his father! It was alive! He watched, amazed, as the still picture of Martus Bain become fluid, a moving, talking man inside the great wooden frame.

"Yes, it's me," said his father, and smiled down gently at him. He had been young when the portrait was painted, not much older than Telius was now, and it was strange to see this vital, dark-haired man speak in his father's voice.

"Am I dreaming?" Telius asked.

"Yes. But you must listen, and remember. You are a fine young man, my son, and I know that what you mean to do is for the good of all—but *wait for the girl.* Wait for all of them, and the girl will explain. The warrior is coming to help."

What! Telius peered closer at the image of his father, frowning. "I-I don't understand, Father! What are you talking about?"

Martus Bain smiled. "I love you, my son. Remember . . ."

"Father? Wait, don't go—" Telius reached upward as the image slowly lost dimension, fading back into paint on canvas, a portrait.

He opened his eyes again, suddenly awake—*truly* awake. He got to his feet, then stepped up to the painting, touching the dried pigments with a shaking hand. It had been a dream, all a dream . . . but it had seemed so *real*!

Telius shook his head, taking a step back from the portrait. *Wait for a girl? The warrior will help?* It didn't make any sense!

He peered closely at the picture. "Father?"
No answer.

Telius smiled nervously at himself, thinking of his earlier wish and feeling a bit foolish. Paintings *did* talk, perhaps, but only in dreams . . .

He had overworked himself, that was all, and he hadn't slept enough in the past weeks. And he had dozed in front of his father's portrait, and dreamed that it spoke a bunch of dream-words, the strange and often absurd conversations that sleep always seemed to bring. Wait for a girl and a warrior! Nonsense, really—but no surprise, considering how tired he'd been lately.

Already, the dream seemed hazy around the edges, the clearness of it becoming clouded by his rational mind—except for the part when his father had told him to remember how much he loved him. That he would keep, because he knew it to be true—and although he knew it was just a dream, it had been good to hear those words again.

"I won't forget," he said, and smiled up at the still portrait. "I love you, too. And I'm going to make you proud, you'll see."

Telius bowed to the portrait and then walked away, nodding to himself. A strange but pleasant dream, and that was all—but once the ritual was past, he'd have to keep his eyes open for a warrior and a girl, just in case.

After a full week of travel, they were all exhausted. Xena knew that she was pushing them, perhaps a bit hard, but the days were passing quickly and there wasn't much time.

Neither Gabrielle nor Alesandra had complained about the rapid pace, but she could see in the tightness of their faces; the toll it was taking—heading out before dawn, not stopping until well after dark. The journey had been uneventful except for when it rained one night; they had passed no more towns and hadn't seen anyone since Osetus, for which

Xena was thankful. They simply didn't have the time to linger over a conversation or rest in the comfort of a warm village inn.

Gabrielle, Gods bless her, had worked hard to keep all of their spirits up—telling stories, joking with Alesandra, and carefully avoiding any talk of the dangers that might wait for them at Avernus. Xena was glad to have her along, and was reminded once again of how valuable Gabrielle was to her—the young woman couldn't fight worth a hoot and often got herself into trouble, but she had a consistent sweetness and lightness of spirit that made traveling with her a pleasure.

Alesandra had proved to be a fine traveler herself, keeping a brave and smiling face turned to the road ahead. She had surprised both Xena and Gabrielle with a delightful singing voice, a high, lilting birdlike sound that rang clear and strong when she sang harmony with Gabrielle. Gabrielle had already taught her every song she knew, and even Xena had joined in once or twice, her rich, deep vocals adding to the pleasant sound.

On the eighth day of their hurried travel, they had stopped for lunch, a quick meal of dried meat and the last of the nuts they had traded for from the woodfolk. Xena only hunted for dinner, because then they had time to cook over a fire, and they usually ate the leftovers for their morning meal. Which made lunch the least favorite break of the day—tough jerky and water, for the most part, supplemented by whatever Gabrielle scrounged up while walking or what bits of dried food they discovered in their packs.

Xena didn't mind eating in the saddle, but she knew that Gabrielle and Alesandra needed the short break; they could spare a few minutes, at least. They had made good time in the last week, and Xena expected to reach Avernus in another five days—arriving the day before the full moon, gods willing . . .

Gabrielle and Alesandra sat on a large stone by the rutted trail, chewing at dried jerky and surveying the woods around them. In the last few days, the forests they'd passed through had thinned, grown sparse and dry. Xena had even said that the hunting was poor, and although she always managed to find dinner, Gabrielle wondered how much longer that would last. It was as if they were traveling toward a place that wouldn't sustain life, and with each day, the surroundings gave them proof—the trees she looked at now weren't just dried out, they seemed sick and stunted. The air was dry, parched, and almost odorless, carrying no scent of earth or wood. There weren't any flowers or berries, and the plants all looked *weird*, like they were from some other world . . .

Alesandra leaned against her and then smiled. "You're right, everything *does* seem strange."

Gabrielle stopped chewing and swallowed, hard. She stared at Alesandra. "You can read minds, too?"

Alesandra grinned. "Not in this case. You're looking at everything around us like it's from a different planet or something—although I *did* get a feeling from you this morning, right after breakfast, when you brushed out my hair. Sometimes I can tell things by touching."

Gabrielle's eyes widened. "Really? You felt something about *me*?"

Alesandra nodded. "I remind you of your little sister, Lila. You worry about her sometimes—but I could tell she was okay, that she's been doing all right and she's not hurt or anything."

Gabrielle smiled, and felt a weight lift off her chest that she hadn't even known was there. "Thank you so much! But how—where was—did you *see* her?"

Alesandra shook her head. "It's not like that. I think . . . I think that when people care about someone, they carry a little piece of that person in their heart. And sometimes they can feel that person, kind of get an idea of how they are—do you know what I mean?"

Gabrielle nodded slowly. "Yes, I think so."

"So sometimes I can get that feeling *through* someone. If there had been something wrong with Lila, I would have known. Because *you* would have known, in your heart."

Gabrielle nodded again. "That makes sense. Can you do it whenever you want?"

"No, I can't control it . . ." Alesandra frowned for a moment, then looked over at Xena, who was standing a few paces away, drinking water. "Something you said in Osetus, Xena—I've been thinking about it."

Xena walked over to join them. "What was that?"

"After that fight—you told Saji that maybe their god, Ling, was the one who had told me about that lady's child. Do you believe in Ling?"

Xena shrugged. "Actually, I was just trying to make a point that they would understand."

Alesandra looked at her, searching Xena's gaze with her own. "So which god is the most powerful? Which one do you believe in?"

Xena crouched down beside her, uncertain

of how to answer. "I don't know, Alesandra. I have heard of many gods and goddesses, and everyone who worships believes that their god is the greatest. All I know is that I have seen some amazing things in my life, and that there are forces far more powerful than man at work in the world—putting a name to such forces wouldn't change them, so I don't choose to seek a name. It is what it is; I believe *that*."

Alesandra frowned again. "That's not really an answer."

Xena stood up, smiling. "For some things, there are no answers. Sometimes when people believe too much in something, they stop looking for any more truth—like the people of Osetus, for instance. Accepting that there may not be an answer to something frees your mind; it allows you to see farther than others, to continue seeking the truth that makes the most sense to *you*."

Alesandra smiled back at her. "Okay. I can understand that."

"Good. And that's enough philosophy for the day, I think. We have to get moving if we want to cover some ground before it gets too dark."

Gabrielle and Alesandra both groaned good-naturedly and stood up, stretching and gathering their things. Xena passed around the leather water pouch and then secured it to Argos's saddle, feeling the ache of the long ride in her lower back. When this was over, she was going to find an inn somewhere with good ale and food and settle into a nice, hot bath—

A noise in the woods.

"Someone's coming," Xena said calmly, not wanting to alarm Alesandra. She drew her sword but held it down low. "Get behind me."

Gabrielle grabbed Alesandra's hand and pulled her behind Xena, who faced the direction of the crashing sound, to the right and in front of them—the noise of one man or woman approaching, not bothering to hide his or her arrival.

Xena didn't know what to expect, but it wasn't the wizened old man who stepped out from behind a close group of trees a second later, dressed in patched leathers and grinning broadly at them. And when he spoke, she was even more surprised.

"Goin' to the Great Dark, are ye?" he rasped, and then grinned wider, baring a mouth full of worn and yellowed teeth. "Avernus it is! Fine, fine! 'Tis a fine place to visit, mebbe, but don't go to live!"

He cackled loudly, and with that laugh, Xena realized two things: The old man wasn't a physical threat—he was too small and ancient to attack them—

—and he was also stark raving mad.

13

The strange old fellow hopped to the road in front of them, and Xena saw that he carried no weapon. She sheathed her sword and smiled at him, raising her hands to show that they meant no harm.

"Hello," she said, and then motioned Gabrielle and Alesandra to step forward with her. "My name is Xena, and these are my friends, Gabrielle and Alesandra—"

The old man's lined and dirty face melted into an expression of gleeful surprise. "Xena! The warrior woman, I heard of ye! Ye're a story I heard! Men be travelin' through, years ago, said Xena was a mighty slayer!"

The odd little man danced around in a circle, delighted with himself, dust rising from his tattered clothes. "I met the great Xena!

Truth, is truth! Ol' Binjer met great Xena—
no one can said it ain't so!"

Xena relaxed a little more. He was insane,
all right—but not in a dangerous way, it
seemed. He wasn't threatening in the
slightest, dancing and cackling to himself
with the open smile of a child.

"So you're . . . Binjer?"

He stopped, out of breath, and nodded eagerly, his rheumy eyes twinkling. " 'Tis
truth! I be Binjer, hunter of rabbit and squir-
rel, fisher of frogs and baker of bread! That's
me! Lived here most my life, not a week out
from the Great Dark!"

Xena nodded. "Is that what you call Hades?"

Binjer's childish grin faded a bit. "Aye.
That an' Avernus. They be the Great Dark,
the black places. Been there once. Wouldn't
go again, not me . . . You neither, aye? Don't
be goin' to the Dark, ain't no good there."

He grinned again, and stepped closer. "Stay
here an' I'll make bread, yes I will! You an'
yer girls is welcome with Binjer!"

As he moved closer to them, Xena could see
that he was very old, more ancient than anyone she had met personally. The average life
of a man wasn't much more than sixty, and
Binjer had that beat by at least twenty years.

He was sprightly, though, and seemed to be in good health.

Perhaps being a few arrows short of a quiver has its benefits, she thought mildly, and then shook her head in apology.

"I'm sorry, Binjer, but we have urgent business farther along. Maybe on the way back—"

He frowned, the crinkles of his face almost swallowing his bright eyes. "Ain't no one come back from the Great Dark! Stay now— bread, I say—and I got fresh frog meat!"

Xena shook her head again, wincing inwardly at Binjer's idea of a taste treat. "Thank you—but as I say, we have to go."

He grinned again and shrugged. "I can go a few miles along, aye? Just a walk for me, good for the heart! Aye? 'Tis all right?"

Xena glanced at Gabrielle and then Alesandra. They both nodded, smiling, obviously agreeable to the idea. A break from routine for them . . . and she *was* curious—how did he know they were going to Hades? And what had he seen on his single visit to Avernus? Xena turned back to a hopeful-looking Binjer and nodded.

"All right. We would be glad to have your company—for a few miles."

Binjer laughed and clapped his hands, then danced around in another small circle, almost singing the words: "Binjer goes with Xena, Xena and her friends!"

Xena grinned, suddenly glad that they had happened upon the old man. Alesandra and Gabrielle both clapped their hands when he finally stopped his dancing, and the four of them started walking, the mad Binjer smiling happily at his newfound friends.

"So how *did* you know we were going to Avernus?" Gabrielle asked.

Binjer grinned his broken smile. "Only place this road leads, ain't it? There's other roads, yes, but this be the one that takes ye straight there." He glanced at Xena and Alesandra, then back to Gabrielle and added, "Besides, ye all got that *look*."

"Look?"

Binjer nodded, then set his face in a grim, determined expression, staring straight ahead. He squared his shoulders and raised his chin, puffing his scrawny chest out.

Gabrielle smirked. "I get it. We look like we're on a mission, right?"

Binjer grinned again, a more natural look for him. The sham of seriousness hadn't suited him. "Truth, 'tis truth! A mission, and one ye don't look forward to, neither! Ol' Binjer sees 'em all, all those men and women that pass me by. I can tell. And I don't see many of 'em come back through, neither. Thems that does, that don't have that look no more, aye . . ."

Xena was riding Argos again, the others walking alongside. It had been almost an hour since they'd met, and the afternoon sun was heavy in the west, the air hot and still. Binjer had already proven himself useful; besides telling some truly awful jokes and merrily singing along with Alesandra and Gabrielle, he'd pointed out a kind of berry that grew in this region, one that none of the others had seen before. The fruits were mottled green, blending into the leaves of the bushes, and they were sweet and plentiful. Gabrielle had already picked a bag full, and Binjer had sworn up and down that they made the best wine he'd ever tasted.

"I may be dim, but I ain't a liar," he said happily, prompting Xena to take a closer look at him. When he wasn't grinning or frowning, the lines of his face seemed to melt away, making him look like an untroubled man. The wrinkles of his skin were from age, not worry or heavy thinking; he'd been born a little slow, she figured, and had apparently lived most of his life alone; no wonder he was a few coins short. He'd had to learn how to keep himself amused.

"Binjer," Xena said gently. "You said you'd been to Avernus once, and to Hades—what was it like?"

Binjer looked up at her and frowned, his lips pursing. "Bad, bad, *bad*. That lake ain't got no fish. No hunting in the woods there, neither, just ugly black birds, *caw! Caw!* Like that."

"Crows," said Gabrielle. Binjer nodded, still frowning as he continued.

"That be Avernus. And then in the castle, that's where Hades be. I seen the wall, 'tis truth! Wouldn't step inside, no—"

Xena felt her pulse speed up. "Castle?"

"Aye, where Bain was. Martus Bain, nice, good man. He and his wife and son—the lady died, though, sad to say, long time ago."

"Martus Bain, the scholar?" At Binjer's confused look, Xena rephrased the question. "The man who studies books?"

Binjer grinned. "That's the one! He'd be old now, mebbe. Older than me, mebbe, and that's *old*!"

Xena was suddenly *delighted* that Binjer had joined them; she knew of Martus Bain— he was from a village near where she had grown up, and she still remembered stories from her childhood about the man who was a counsel to kings. Bain had written books on everything from warfare to penmanship, and had been widely renowned for his intelligence and scholarship.

He had disappeared when she was still a young woman, and stories had it that he had married and become a recluse, hiding away somewhere to devote himself to his studies . . .

Hiding in a castle near Avernus, perhaps? Xena nodded to herself, and could almost hear the pieces falling into place. Although she had never met the man, he was said to be a fighter for good; could it be that he had chosen a place so close to Hades in order to study the place, perhaps to try and unravel the mysteries of its darker side?

"When was the last time you were at this castle, Binjer?"

The old man cocked his head to one side. "Oh, not so long. Well—a few years, I guess. Mebbe ten? Martus was old, yes, but his son was yer age, I think." He nodded at Alesandra.

Gabrielle and Alesandra exchanged looks with Xena and each other. Xena could see that they were coming to the same conclusions.

"A *young* man with no evil in his heart—" said Gabrielle.

"—who has a book—a book of spells?" said Xena.

"Who will not heed his father's words," said Alesandra softly, and she finished for them. "This young man makes a mistake with this book, and he undoes a beast that *allows* evil into the world."

"Cerebrus," said Xena, "the guard at the gate." All three of them stared at one another.

Binjer gazed at them, smiling, and then laughed. "Hey, that's a good one! I got a story about a king that loses his pants and the whole kingdom goes around without *their* pants, just to be fashion-like! Can you picture such a thing?"

Xena turned to him. "Binjer, can you show us where this castle is? It's very important that we find it."

A look of unease flashed across his pleasant old face. "No, I not be goin' to Avernus no more . . . but say, I could draw ye a map, I guess! That would be good, aye?"

Xena smiled at Binjer, and his expression went back to one of simple happiness.

"That would be fine, just fine," she said. "Maybe you can join us for dinner, and you could show us then."

Binjer grinned and broke into another

dance. "Eat with Xena, and her friends! Show them where the castle stands!"

Xena smiled for him, but felt an overwhelming urgency to get to Avernus. The moon would be full soon, and in this instance, figuring out the puzzle didn't mean that it was solved.

Martus Bain's son was going to open the gates to Hades, and unless they could stop him in time, his actions would bring about the doom of their world.

They camped early, so that Binjer would have time to find his way home before it got too dark. Using a stick in the dirt, he drew a simple map to the castle, apparently only a few hours from Avernus. In spite of the childish drawing, the directions were clear and Xena thought they could find it easily.

Binjer exclaimed over Gabrielle's roasting of the two rabbits that Xena had caught for dinner. "This be better'n frog, 'tis truth! I can say to anyone, Xena found rabbit an' Gabrielle cooked 'em good! Dinner for Binjer, ain't that nice?"

When they had finished eating, they all stood to wish their strange companion a safe trip home. Alesandra even hugged him, and smiled up at him with a light in her eyes.

"You won't be lonely for long, Binjer," she said, and hugged him again. "You'll be with new friends soon."

Xena and Gabrielle glanced at each other and then bid their own farewells. Binjer made them promise to come visit him when they came back from their quest.

"You can try my wine, the *best*," he said, and with another big grin, he turned and walked away, singing to himself. A few minutes later, there was only the sound of crickets, warming up to their own twilight music.

Gabrielle looked over at Alesandra. "Did you 'see' something when you touched him?"

Alesandra nodded. "Yes. He's going to be moving soon, although I didn't see where. But the people there will like him, and he'll be happy."

Xena studied Binjer's map for another moment, fixing the image firmly in her mind, and then joined the other two by the crackling fire. She gave them a brief account of what she knew about Martus Bain.

"It all makes sense, doesn't it?" said Gabrielle. "At least we know what we're up against now. It doesn't sound like this Bain character *means* to do anything wrong; that's something, isn't it?"

Xena nodded, but suddenly remembered a phrase that she had heard many times throughout her life. "The road to Hades is paved with good intentions," she said, and then shrugged. "Meaning well is a fine thing—but it's the action taken that matters most in the end."

All three of them considered that silently, watching the flames dance in the gathering night—where the moon rose cold and high, almost full now.

14

The journey had taken longer than they'd expected. It was the night before the full moon, which meant they had less than twenty-four hours—and they still hadn't seen the waters of Avernus. Or much of anything, for that matter.

The days and nights passed faster than Argos could travel, even if he had been able to carry all three of them. The war-horse, though in his prime, could not have borne the extra weight for such a journey—no horse could have. Xena and Alesandra rode, while Gabrielle hurried alongside; Gabrielle never had gotten the hang of riding easily. The large animal, though nice enough, just made her nervous.

Not as nervous as this place does; Gabrielle

thought worriedly. *Or that moon.* It *looked* full as it rose heavy into the night sky, and although Xena said she was sure that they would find the castle at first light the next morning, Gabrielle had seen the concern in her usually unreadable pale eyes. Even looking up at the nearly round orb now made Gabrielle's heart pound. What if Binjer's directions were wrong? What if they *couldn't* find the castle?

"Tomorrow night," said Alesandra. "Tomorrow night it's going to happen."

The girl was also gazing at the moon, looking as scared and exhausted as Gabrielle felt. The surroundings didn't help their moods much, either—never in all her life had Gabrielle seen such a desolate and ugly place. Xena said that it meant they were very close, and they didn't dare travel any farther after dark or they would risk the nightmares that were said to haunt the area.

This place *is a nightmare,* thought Gabrielle. She and Alesandra sat close to the fire, waiting for Xena to return from her hunt. The gnarled, gray trees seemed to come to life by the dying light of day, creeping toward them as twilight faded. She knew it was just her imagination (well, *probably*), but the whole area was . . . *forbidding,* straight-out spooky.

Gabrielle smiled at Alesandra, hoping that she looked more confident than she actually was. "Hey, we're almost there! *Nothing* is going to happen tomorrow night; we'll find the castle, and Xena will explain things to this Bain person, and that'll be it. End of story."

"Maybe," said Alesandra. "I hope so." She didn't sound particularly hopeful.

Gabrielle moved closer to the girl, as much for Alesandra's sake as for her own. This was a place that seemed to suck the hope out of everything, although at least the crows had finally shut up . . .

Every day for a week the landscape had grown stranger, more ominous—the trees, the air, even the quality of light had become like something out of a bad dream, a dream of a desolate emptiness. With each step they took toward Avernus, Gabrielle had discovered some new bizarre feature that made her skin crawl: brittle yellowed grass covered the rocky soil in funguslike patches; the few animals they'd seen peered out at them from behind the knotty trees, their eyes wild and red, almost feral; just the absence of any other human beings was bad enough—but those squawking crows! From sunrise to sundown for two whole days the skies had been filled with their horrible shrieks, like a mocking chorus aimed at their very humanity. *Leave*, those cries seemed to say. *Leave or be lost forever* . . .

Xena stepped into the flickering circle of light so suddenly that Gabrielle jumped, her heart thumping loudly.

"Gods, don't *do* that!"

Xena arched a delicate brow. "It's not my fault that you wouldn't hear anything approaching short of a herd of cattle."

"Yeah, well, you don't have to be so *quiet* all the time," Gabrielle muttered. She noticed that Xena wasn't carrying anything and felt her spirits drop even lower.

"No luck?"

Xena shook her head and reached for their food pack, still on Argos's saddle. "If there's anything alive in these woods, I didn't hear it."

Gabrielle sighed. "Then there isn't anything alive," she said, and then shuddered slightly at the words. Binjer hadn't been exaggerating; except for the crows, the woods near Avernus held no life—yet another unsettling thought to add to her already long list of them.

Xena frowned as she sorted through the last of their supplies. Enough for another full day, if they ate small meals. Beyond that, they'd have to leave the area so that she could hunt.

If we don't find Bain's castle tomorrow; *eating well will be the least of our troubles.* She winced inwardly at the thought and then portioned out one of the last hunks of jerky. It wasn't like her to think so negatively, but in truth, it worried her that they hadn't even reached Avernus yet, let alone the castle. She had underestimated how long it would take them, that was all—but she couldn't help feeling as if they were moving in slow-motion, that no matter how hard they tried, they wouldn't arrive in time . . .

She had considered going out alone while the other two slept, to scout for the lake and the castle—but in spite of the fullness of the moon, the land was treacherously dark, as if the ground were somehow absorbing the light. She didn't want to risk Argos on a scouting mission in these conditions. And besides, it didn't feel safe to leave Gabrielle and Alesandra alone, even for a short time.

She sighed again; it was this place, the air here—hope was an unwelcome thing, she felt it deeply. It was as though they had journeyed into a blasted land, poor in both beauty *and* spirit—and the lack of essence was like a sponge, draining the life from the people who passed through.

Xena sat down across from Gabrielle and Alesandra after handing out their meager supper. They both looked worn out and yet anxious, their faces like mirrors of her own concerns.

"We'll be there tomorrow," said Xena. "Try not to worry overmuch. It won't help matters."

Gabrielle sighed. "Binjer didn't say anything about there being any guards, did he? Will we be stopped?"

Xena shook her head. "No, he didn't say. I doubt there are many, if any at all; the castle would be too isolated to support a large number. And I imagine that once we explain the situation, we'll have no trouble getting in."

Alesandra looked up from the fire. "What if we do, though? What if they try to stop us?"

Xena shrugged. "Stay behind me. I haven't met a man yet who wouldn't stand down at the point of a sword."

Gabrielle smiled. "Oh, really? What about that time—"

"Sorry, let me rephrase that; I've never met a *smart* man who wouldn't stand down at the point of a sword." Xena grinned. "And now that you mention it, I've met quite a few with poor survival skills. If it comes to that, just try and keep out of the way until they . . . gain some wisdom."

Gabrielle nodded. "And once we get inside?"

Xena thought about it. "We find Martus, and talk to him—or his son. Alesandra said that he's not a bad young man, and I know that Martus Bain could not have changed so much, even in twenty years. He was renowned for his kindness as well as his intelligence."

Gabrielle turned to Alesandra. "You said that both you and I needed to be there . . . ?"

Alesandra nodded. "Yes, that was a very strong impression. I still don't know what we're supposed to do, if anything at all—but I know we have to be with Xena when she meets with the younger Bain."

Gabrielle chewed at her lip uneasily. She had hoped that Alesandra would have seen something a bit more specific by now, the roles that they would play in the prophecy, for example—obviously not. That worried her as much as anything else thus far. What if the final outcome somehow depended on what *she* did, or didn't do?

"You'll do fine," said Xena, smiling at her with a glint in her eye.

Gabrielle sighed. How did Xena always

know? She wasn't *that* obvious, was she? Maybe her expressions needed some work . . .

Alesandra dropped her gaze back to the fire. "Sometimes when the outcome of a situation can be changed, my feelings about it change— or they go away altogether. It's happened a couple of times before. Like once, I saw that Otus was going to trip and fall really bad when he was out cutting wood. And when I told him that, he stayed home that day, and the feeling went away. He went the next day instead, and suffered no incident, nothing."

She kept her gaze on the moving flames, her small shoulders hunched. "My feelings about what's going to happen tomorrow have become kind of cloudy, as if things *may* happen differently—although they may not; I can't say for sure. But I still . . . What I said, a couple of weeks ago, about one of us not coming back—that feeling hasn't gone away, or changed. It's gotten *stronger*."

Xena reached out and gently patted her shoulder. "Hey—we're not going into this with our eyes closed. Once we explain the situation to Martus and his son, there won't be any problem . . ."

Alesandra hugged her knees even tighter. "Yes, there will," she said, her voice small and pitiful. "There's going to be trouble. The closer we get, the more I'm sure of it."

She looked up then, and met Xena's eyes, her own despairing and frightfully, painfully young. "*I'm* the one who won't be coming back. I feel it as clearly as I see you now."

15

Telius had probably slept for a total of twenty minutes all night, but he sat up in bed feeling wide awake, his stomach in nervous knots.

"Tonight," he said softly, and instantly it was an endless chant in the back of his mind. *Tonight, tonight, tonight—*

The sun had already risen, the pale morning light filtering through his window as the crows warmed up to their daily song. He'd been raised with their cries, heard them every day since before he could recall, and had become accustomed to tuning the sound out. Today, however, he listened for a moment, really hearing them for the first time in perhaps years. How desolate they sounded, almost mournful . . .

Maybe after tonight, the skies would fill

with different songs, the crows no longer the sole inhabitants of the lands near Avernus. Perhaps, in time, flowers would grow. Animals might come to live here, seeking refuge in the virgin forests of a new era—one of compassion and peaceful freedom for all living things.

Tonight, the birth of it all. Tonight when the moon rises proud and full, casting her light for the last time on the dark world of man! Tomorrow, the sun would awake to find a changed land—and Telius would be responsible for that change. Not for glory or riches, although those things would surely follow—but because he believed, as had his father, that the world *could* be such a place, that humanity had the capability to do away with the evil it tolerated now. All that had been needed was the way, the key to unlock that door to a brighter reality—and he'd found it.

Telius got out of bed slowly, savoring the stretch of his tired muscles. Funny—he had been so impatient for *weeks* now, so eager for this day to come that he'd hardly been able to stand it; and now that it had come, he felt a kind of calm settle over him, in spite of his knotted belly. This was the last day of its kind, maybe forever; why shouldn't it be enjoyed, bid farewell to with some kind of mercy? He was about to create a new existence—and destroy an old one. The least he could do was luxuriate in its final, dying moments.

Telius grinned. "Good-bye, cruel world," he said, and then laughed out loud. The rich, full sound of his pleasure surprised him, and he laughed again; it had been too long since he'd felt so good, so happy with his life, and the proof was that his laughter seemed strange to him, out of place.

Not anymore. Tonight . . . Everything changes tonight.

He walked to his small window, still grinning, and looked out over the courtyard, taking a deep breath of the cool morning air. There was nothing that could dampen his spirits today, no doubts to face—

—the girl will explain—

Telius frowned. Where had *that* come from? He thought about it uncertainly for a moment. The girl . . . and a warrior, that was it! He'd had some kind of dream—maybe a week or so ago? It was hard to remember, he'd been sleeping so erratically; the last few days had kind of blended together . . .

Telius shrugged it off. What was a dream,

when the reality of the full moon was *to-night*?

Nothing. A dream was a *shadow* of nothing.

And yet . . . He frowned again, irritated with this vague dark spot on what would surely prove to be the greatest day of his life. Did he have any doubts that he'd buried in his excitement? Could there be some hidden concern, perhaps?

Telius thought about it, hard, for another moment. And then shook his head.

"No," he said softly. "I'm doing the right thing; I know it."

In spite of his confidence, he somehow didn't feel as happy as he had been only a moment before. Well, he was tired; when the ritual was complete, he'd sleep for a full day, get his mind rested and back to normal. After tonight, he'd have the time to relax.

For now, though, a final breakfast in the old world. He put on a smile, but couldn't shake the feeling that he'd forgotten something, something that might prove to be important . . .

Scowling slightly, Telius dressed and headed for the kitchen, wondering why he wasn't as happy as he should be. And wishing very, very much that his father were there.

• • •

They were up and moving as the first rays of cold dawn broke across the bleak landscape. Both Gabrielle and Alesandra had suffered bad dreams—not as horrific as any of them had feared, but bad enough that no one got much rest. Xena had dozed only lightly, her ears trained to any sound, and the tossings of the other two had kept her from deeper sleep.

As if they didn't have enough to worry over, Alesandra's frightening talk from the night before had cast a pall over everything. Xena hoped that the vision could still change, but it was hard to hope when she looked into the child's mild eyes. Alesandra seemed certain of her own destiny—that when their quest was over, whatever the outcome, she would not be leaving with them. Although she hadn't said anything else about it, Xena could see the sadness in her gaze, the belief there.

Gabrielle was anxious and worried, but Xena acted as though there were still hope— and if Xena could do it, so could she. There was no man or woman alive that she trusted the way she trusted Xena; the warrior had proven herself again and again, and if anyone could change things, she was the one.

They ate quickly and set out, each determined to be brave for the others and each plagued with her own private fears.

Tonight, the prophecy of darkness would come to pass, or pass by. And although the three of them had roles to play in the final unfolding of this fate, in the end only time would tell which path the future would choose.

Xena cursed softly to herself, wishing that she *had* scouted for the lake the night before. Not going had been a mistake, and one that might cost them more than they could afford. Where was it? They'd been moving since dawn, the sun was directly overhead now, and *where was it?* This was no puddle they were searching for, but a decent sized *lake*, the size of a small town—and without finding it to get their bearings, there was no hope of finding Bain's castle.

Although it hardly seemed possible, the lands were even more dismal and grim than before; Xena held that in her mind, the only clue that they hadn't somehow missed Avernus. The ground had set into a series of rolling hills, the only gentle feature of an otherwise desolate landscape—and also frustrating, since at the crest of each mound she searched for Avernus, and found nothing.

The castle is still a few hours past the lake;

if we don't find it soon ... Xena gritted her teeth, leaving the thought unfinished.

The very air about them was a sickly yellow, the only sounds in its stillness those of hundreds upon hundreds of the scavenger black birds; Xena didn't even want to guess at what they survived on in this barren place ...

She could read the growing apprehension in both of the others, the rising alarm as they topped each hill and saw no lake. They reached the top of a hill now and saw only more of the same.

Argos didn't care much for the atmosphere either, and had become a struggle to control with each step forward. The pale steed snorted in unease, maybe sensing the lifelessness around them—or maybe just sick to death of the crows' relentless cries, as she was. Gods, if she never saw another crow, she'd die a happy woman.

Alesandra rode quietly in front of her, as she had all morning, the animation seemingly drained from her small body. When Xena pulled Argos to a halt, the child didn't even bother to ask why; it was as if her hope had fled, leaving her even smaller.

Gabrielle didn't say a word as Xena dismounted and handed her the reins; she had been thinking all morning about Alesandra's vision of her own fate. Could it be possible? Gabrielle didn't even want to consider it, and searched her own instincts again and again for some sign that everything would be all right. Unfortunately, her gut feelings seemed to be on the fritz. In truth, the only thing she *knew* was that Xena would do everything in her power to make things turn out okay; and with that thought, nothing seemed quite as awful. *She* wouldn't want to get in Xena's way—and Bain, if he had the sense that the gods gave a stick of wood, would surely feel the same way.

Xena walked to the edge of the hill and scanned again for Avernus, using all of her training and experience to pick apart what she saw. She closed her eyes for a moment, concentrating on nothing, and then opened them, seeing everything as if for the first time.

There were more crows flocked toward the east. The sickly grasses grew thicker directly in front of them. The trees to the west were mostly smaller, drier than the ones scattered around them now—

She ground her teeth together, wanting to scream. Everything contradicted everything else! According to her own eyes, the lake was in every direction but the one they chose. She was exhausted, frustrated, almost overwhelmed with the pressure of their need to find Avernus, and find it quickly—

A gentle touch on her arm, and Xena looked down to see Alesandra standing beside her, one small, pale hand lightly resting against the warrior's tanned skin. Xena opened her mouth to say something, and then stopped; where Alesandra touched her, her arm tingled.

Xena closed her eyes again, searching for the lake, replaying what her expert senses had given her to work with.

When she opened them again, Alesandra was smiling. And pointing.

"It's that way," she said, motioning roughly southeast.

Xena smiled back, suddenly knowing that it *was* that way. Alesandra had found what Xena had known but had been unable to get to in her frustration.

And perhaps more importantly, Alesandra had found hope again, for all of them.

16

It was another two hours before they reached the lake, but Alesandra had seen with Xena's thoughts correctly; it had been to the south-east. They easily could have lost hours searching for it without Alesandra's help.

Xena knew that they didn't have time to linger, but they paused for a moment anyway, in spite of their hurry—or perhaps because of it. It was surprisingly lovely, an oasis of beauty in a blighted land. The shores were bare, but the waters were calm, reflecting the afternoon light in shades of brilliance, a deep blue-green tint at the surface. Just looking at it helped Xena to feel grounded again, her center back in place.

Gabrielle sighed. "It's a relief to see something around here that isn't ugly."

Alesandra nodded, as did Xena; she had kept Argos back from the edge, worried that despite its loveliness, the lake might be poisoned. As she watched, however, she noted several crows dip into the water at various spots around the shore, bathing and drinking. Xena led the thirsty horse down to the lake and let him take his fill before they moved on.

Binjer had said three hours to reach the castle from Avernus, maybe more. Which meant that they should arrive at sunset or just before, assuming his directions were right.

And less than an hour after the sun goes down, the moon will rise, thought Xena. She didn't like it; they were going to be cutting it much closer than she would have chosen; of course, *she* would have chosen for Alesandra never to have had the damned vision in the first place, given her *choice. If wishes were horses . . .*

There was nothing to be done for it; they had done their best so far, and that was all they could do now.

That, and pray that Bain's son wasn't an impatient man.

Telius paced the lower chamber, occasionally stopping to ponder the wall that Hades hid behind. It was the third time he'd come down today, his earlier thoughts of lingering good-byes to the old world long forgotten. He wanted this day to draw to a close, for the sun to set, for the moon to be high and full at once, sooner—

He gazed at the high wall, his eyes moving over the rune patterns and the strange words engraved in the stones. Concepts of evil and good, of the spaces between . . . What things would he see behind these symbols? The entrance to Hades was supposed to be like a corridor, guarded by the three-headed dog; would it be cold and dark, echoing with the cries of the tortured? Or as silent and lonely as a crypt, with only a lingering scent of ancient perfume, the smell of pomegranate? Would Cerebrus die painfully, or simply fade into nothingness? And once he was destroyed, would the souls of saints in transit be a visible wave, coursing out through the gate to redeem the world? Or only a presence of goodness . . . ?

"Perhaps once destroyed, this place will be at peace," he whispered aloud. He longed to speak the words that would alter this gate, to feel the powers of the higher universe channeling through him . . .

"As soon as the moon comes into view,"

he added, clenching his jaw. Only a few more hours, and it seemed like a lifetime. He started to pace again, already amending his spoken statement—the *second* the moon came into view, he would begin the ritual.

His father's memory deserved no less.

They were making very good time; Xena was pleased with their progress, and thought that they would arrive well before the sun set. The stones and trees that they passed were already casting longer shadows, a constant reminder of the need to keep up their steady pace.

Xena held Argos in an easy trot, and Gabrielle, though winded, insisted that there was no need to slow down.

"I'm fine," she panted, jogging alongside Xena and Alesandra. "Really."

Xena nodded, grinning at her. "Right. As soon as you tire, we'll switch places. I don't want you to collapse before we get there—"

Argos suddenly stumbled, and then stopped, favoring his left foreleg.

Xena took a deep breath. *It's nothing, a long shadow; he didn't see another rock.*

She dismounted quickly, clucking her tongue against her teeth to soothe the uneasy horse. She helped Alesandra off and then crouched down, still hoping fervently that he had simply misstepped—

He'd thrown a shoe. Their ride from Avernus had been a rocky one, and he must have kicked it off against a stone.

Alesandra and Gabrielle turned worried gazes to her, and Xena silently cursed herself for not visiting a blacksmith when she last had the chance—it would take too long if she started cursing aloud, and they didn't have the time to spare. She knew how to shod him herself, but without a shoe and the proper tools, the situation was hopeless.

"We can't ride him," said Xena, shaking her head slowly. "He might split the hoof, and without a salve to stave off an infection, it could kill him."

All three of them surveyed the dismal lands around them, the shadows seeming to grow with each blink of the eye.

"What do we do?" Gabrielle turned her wide-eyed, anxious gaze back to Xena. Alesandra chewed at her lip nervously.

Xena sighed. She looked in the direction where the castle lay and then back at the alarmed girls.

"We hurry," she said quietly. "And hope that the moon takes her time tonight."

• • •

Telius was in his room again, watching through his window as the sun dipped slowly to the west, the crows still barking out their sorrowful cries. He sat on the edge of his bed, the book resting in his lap, open to the ritual that his father had surely sought for so long.

Again, his mood had changed. Strange, how in all this eternal day he'd gone from reflective to excited to anxious, again and again. It was as if his brain couldn't sit still either—and he was surprised to find himself feeling something else now, something that he couldn't quite put a name to . . .

His hands shook slightly, rattling the brittle pages of the ancient book, musty with secrets. His body had run on adrenaline for too long; he needed to sleep, but knew that there was no way his mind would let him, not now—and he didn't want to, anyway. It was all too close now.

He felt on edge, nervous with anticipation, and he was so exhausted that he didn't know what to make of the thoughts running through his head. What if something went wrong? What if the spell didn't work the way it was supposed to, or he mispronounced something and damaged the effectiveness?

Telius couldn't place the feeling, because in all of the weeks of planning and dreaming, it was the one thing he had never expected to feel—and he couldn't acknowledge it now, because to do so might change his actions, and there was no way that he was going to betray his father in such a way. Not his father, and not himself.

Telius was worried. And somewhere down deep, he was also afraid.

The sun dropped lower into the sky as he read the spell yet again. It wouldn't be long now.

"There it is! That's the castle!"

Gabrielle pointed eagerly toward the pile of stones, half-hidden by a cluster of trees, only a few hundred paces ahead of them. The sun was gone, the sky thick with twilight, but they still had time, maybe an hour. Maybe.

Xena set Alesandra down and quickly checked Argos's unshod hoof for any damage; it was intact. They looked at the castle, remembering that Binjer had said it looked like a ruin; he hadn't exaggerated even a bit. With the tumbled piles of stones all around and the shadows of the trees against it, it barely seemed whole.

They'd made it. Gabrielle could hardly believe it, after all of the trials of their long journey—the last few hours in particular. They had half-run, half-walked for a seemingly endless amount of time, Xena carrying Alesandra when she couldn't keep up, Argos stumbling along with them as the sun had slowly gone down.

They hurried toward the castle now, the seconds ticking painfully by, each of them feeling the pressure of time lost. Stones, bigger and more solidly hewn, the loosely spaced forest of twisted trees—and then the gate, finally, they were at the gate; their destination reached after so many days of travel, so many hard days: the castle near Avernus, of Alesandra's prophecy, seemingly from so long ago.

There were no guards, or at least none that they could see. They found a low-limbed tree near the entrance and hitched Argos there, moving quickly and quietly.

Xena motioned at them to be silent as she listened for a moment to the shaded twilight, cocking her head to catch any sounds of movement. From somewhere beyond the gate, she heard a shuffling of multiple feet— from the sound, too small to be human. The Bains obviously kept livestock in their courtyard, but apparently no guards—no *human* guards at all.

Which means there's a keystone, she thought, and turned to Alesandra and Gabrielle. "No one," she said quietly. "I want you to check all along this wall and around the gate for a keystone; it will probably be a small rock, big as the tip of my thumb—either sticking out from the rest or sunken in a little. Look carefully, and don't push on it if you find it, just tell me."

Within a minute, Alesandra called out to them in a loud and excited whisper, from right next to the gate. She was kneeling near the base of the heavy door. "Here! There's— Wait, there are . . . *four* of them?"

"Don't touch them," said Xena, hurrying over. Alesandra stepped back as Xena crouched down to inspect the stones. One was set high, the others in a triangle pattern beneath it.

The top one was probably the key to the gate, but the others? Xena scowled, wishing that she only had human guards to deal with after all. She'd seen something like this once before, at a small keep that she and her army had wanted to get into, ages past; the stones were set up to trigger off mechanical weapons or traps. A very efficient way to keep intruders from getting very far once past the gate. Four of her best men had been seriously injured before she'd been able to call off that attack . . .

Before, however, she hadn't known. She remembered learning afterward that the stones had to be pushed in a particular order to deactivate whatever traps were set.

She pressed the top stone, and the gate creaked open, just enough to get a hand through. At least she was right about *that*. Alesandra and Gabrielle grinned at each other as Xena continued to study the arrangement.

"Alesandra, come look at these and tell me if you get any feelings from them. Look for some kind of pattern."

The child bent down to look, gently resting one hand against the rocks. She closed her eyes for a moment, then opened them, shaking her head. "No, nothing."

Gabrielle looked at them, too, but had no idea what they even meant. The gate was *open* already, what did it matter?

Xena sighed, then stood up. "I'm going to go in first, and I want you both to wait here. Those stones are hooked up to traps, probably just inside the courtyard. If we knew the right pattern, we could disarm the traps—but we don't, and I don't want to mess with them randomly; it could set them all off at once."

Gabrielle frowned. "Maybe we should try and reason it out, you know—if we could figure out something about the design of the castle . . ."

She trailed off, realizing that this would take time that they didn't have to spare. The sun was fully gone now, the last of its light quickly fading from the dusky air. The moon would be peeking over the horizon in a matter of moments, although it wouldn't be completely in view for a bit longer . . .

But maybe not long enough. Maybe we don't even have the moments anymore.

Gabrielle nodded, and put her arm around Alesandra's shoulders, the girl looking at Xena with frightened eyes.

"Be careful," said Gabrielle softly, and Xena smiled, drawing her sword.

"I will. I'll come back for you as soon as it's clear."

Without another word, Xena edged past the heavy door and stepped cautiously into the dim courtyard, all of her senses on full alert, her sword at the ready.

She waited a few seconds, then warily put one foot forward, looking to each shadow, checking anywhere that might conceal a danger. Nothing, yet . . .

Another step. Another. Between each, she had to wait, uncertain as to what the darkness held. It was getting *too* dark; they didn't have the time for this—but there was no other way. Xena took another step—

—and something hurtled toward her out of the shadows at incredible speed.

17

Telius waited until the last of the sun's waning rays crept away and then left his room, *A Histore of Nether* clenched in one trembling hand. The moon wouldn't be up for another hour, but an edge of it would be showing in only twenty minutes or so. He would go to the underground chamber and meditate for a short while, preparing himself for the ritual—and when he was sure that enough time had passed, he would light the candles and begin.

The cold, dark hallways echoed back each footstep, the sounds filling the silence of his deserted home. When he was halfway down the final hall, he paused a moment, thinking that he'd heard something outside—but as the last of his own echoes died away, he couldn't detect any sound.

"Imagination," he murmured, and the darkness stole the word away, leaving only silence again. Telius shook his head and continued on, as nervous and excited as his tired mind could allow. Just to make sure that he wouldn't be interrupted, he paused at the final junction and armed the indoor traps. He rarely used them, but the extra insurance would give him peace of mind as he prepared.

He was ready, as ready as the world was to rid itself of evil. Nothing could stop him now.

Xena dropped flat in a single motion as a score of sharpened spears shot out of the darkness.

They whistled overhead, the lowest of them missing her by scant inches. She turned her head, and watched them clatter against the stone wall opposite and fall to the ground.

Moving slowly, carefully, she sat up and searched the packed dirt around her feet. Brushing the dried soil away, she found the trigger—a square stone set into the dirt that depressed slightly when she touched it. She could hear the mechanism in the wall, the grating of rock against rock; when she'd stepped on the hidden trigger, the cocked spears had been loosed.

She stood up from where she'd dropped to the ground and scanned the floor of the courtyard, looking for other traps. Precious moments ticked by, but she couldn't be hurried; to miss one could mean death, and she was needed alive to stop Alesandra's prophecy. There had been three keystones, which probably meant three devices . . .

There, another one, ahead and to her right! The dirt was cracked around the edges of the trigger, a circular stone this time.

Xena turned slowly, her sword raised again. If she found the third by accident, she could use the weapon as a defense, slashing at whatever came . . .

Her trained eyes focused on the cracked shape of the third, and she lowered her blade, grinning.

"Gabrielle, Alesandra! Come in, and walk straight toward me!"

The two of them were only pale shapes in the dark yard, and they moved quickly, eager to be reunited. When they reached her, Xena pointed out the stones, making certain that both of them saw the triggers clearly.

"Let's go," said Xena, and they carefully moved toward what looked like the main opening, Alesandra clutching Gabrielle's hand. When they reached the dark entrance, Xena saw another set of keystones in the frame, identical to the ones at the front gate.

She nodded; of course, the traps would be useless if you couldn't arm them from inside as well . . .

She looked closer, peering down at the stones. It was too dark to see clearly, but—

Beneath the set rocks was another design of raised keystones, this one different than the others. There were five of them—but they could only mean one thing.

Somewhere inside the castle, there were five more traps, probably as deadly as the first, ready and waiting to stop them.

Telius sat cross-legged amid the unlit candles, his eyes closed. He had found his center, a meditative technique that Martus had taught him long ago, focusing his energies on an area a hand's span below his navel. From here, he breathed deeply, drawing the air in and holding it a few beats before letting it go.

With each breath exhaled, he let tension escape; with each drawn in, he felt the cool energy of the world's goodness fill him up. His mind was clear, his body still, his spirit at peace—the prerequisites for casting a spell of this magnitude.

Telius drew in another deep breath and then let it out slowly and opened his eyes.

It was time.

Xena held up one hand, stopping Alesandra and Gabrielle from stepping inside.

"Oh, *no*," said Gabrielle miserably. "Not again."

Xena craned her neck around the edge of the doorway, looking up and down the dark corridor. Which way? They couldn't afford to get lost, and there was no time for her to search all of the passages for triggers—

Beside her, Alesandra suddenly swooned, leaning hard against Gabrielle. The girl had gone pale, her eyes far away.

"It's beginning," she whispered, and she turned her distant gaze up to Xena. "The candles are lit . . ."

Xena grabbed her cold hand. "Alesandra, *where is he!*"

Alesandra clenched her eyes tightly, and when she opened them, Xena could see the horrible fear there.

"That way," she said, and pointed to the left.

Xena didn't hesitate. She drew her sword again, and stepped into the shadowy hall. "Stay close! Watch my feet, and follow them with your own, both of you! Gabrielle, you bring up the rear, help Alesandra if she needs it—now, carefully!"

The passage was too dark to see the triggers, and there wasn't enough time to move too slowly. Xena could only hope that if they hit one, it would be aimed for her—and that the injury wouldn't kill her.

Together, they moved into the darkness.

Telius stood in the circle surrounded by flickering candles and opened the book to the marked page. In a deep, clear voice, he began to read.

Halfway down the corridor, Xena felt a slight shift beneath her right foot.

"Hold still!" she shouted, and then felt the floor open up, the stones falling out from under her.

She bent her knees and then leapt, pushed hard against the crumbling rocks. She held the sword high, gripped both the handle and the flat of the blade at once, using it as a focal point.

—*legs up tuck*—

Xena somersaulted over the sword, and stumbled backward when she landed, her heels finding only empty air. She shifted forward to the balls of her feet, leaning into the movement—

—and stepped onto solid ground again. She

turned, and saw that Alesandra and Gabrielle were safe, huddled together across the open pit.

Smart, very smart; whoever had designed this castle had known their stuff. Xena looked down into the trap, but the shadows were too dense to see where it ended.

"Gabrielle, can you make it?" Xena asked. The pit was about three paces across, a good-sized leap.

Gabrielle stepped to the edge and then nodded.

Xena sheathed her sword and then stepped to the rim on her side. "Alesandra, this is going to be scary, but you'll be okay. Gabrielle is going to throw you over to me—"

Alesandra stepped away. "I— Do we have to?"

Xena nodded. "It's okay. I won't let you fall, all right? Just hold very still."

Xena looked at Gabrielle, who nodded back, then smiled at Alesandra. "I'm pretty strong, so don't worry," Gabrielle said.

She picked Alesandra up easily and then started rocking back and forth, letting Alesandra's weight carry the movement. The child squeezed her eyes closed.

Gabrielle counted as she swung her. "One— two—*three!*"

She threw Alesandra into the air, over the yawning black pit, and Xena reached out—

—and caught her. The child clutched at Xena's neck, but she didn't cry or scream. Alesandra's bravery was truly amazing.

"I've got you, shh," Xena whispered, and then set her down gently. "Let's help Gabrielle, okay?"

Alesandra let go, nodding. They stood to either side as Gabrielle backed away from the trap and, with a determined look on her face, charged forward, jumping just as she reached the edge.

She flew across the pit easily, landing on her feet several paces past the rim, and was so surprised at her success that she promptly fell to the floor, giving her tailbone a good whack.

Gabrielle stood up, grinning and flushed. "I guess I made it."

Xena nodded. "That you did. Come on."

They started forward again, Xena in the lead. She talked softly as they walked, keeping her senses trained for the trigger stones.

"There were five keystones, but it stands to reason that the traps are all over the castle, not just where we are—if we're lucky, that was the only one we'll find . . ."

They reached the end of the corridor, where

they could go either left or right. Alesandra pointed to the right. Xena could see the flickering light of a torch somewhere ahead, past a corner farther along. Bain must have lit a few of them, to find his way to and from the gate.

"We have to hurry, Xena! He's already started speaking, I can feel it. We can't let him finish!"

Xena nodded and stepped forward—

—and felt a stone shift under her foot.

Telius read from the long list of words, looking up often to see what happened.

". . . aldas, yerick, danetus, circt . . ."

Was the air getting colder?

". . . phelon, tirered . . ."

A glance to the wall, and then back to the words, but he felt his heart speed up at what he saw. A veil of mist, thickening, covering the runes and clouding the inscriptions.

". . . giatel, iestus . . ."

A look. The wall was completely hidden behind the gray mist. He read on, reaching the last of the magical words, his voice rising with excitement.

". . . haestra, lumn, rioxedela, shualdub!"

Telius's eyes widened as the room was filled with a great noise, a sound unlike any he'd ever heard. A deep, moaning cry, both human and inhuman at once and almost deafening in its clamor.

The misty cloud formed and unformed, drifting away into nothingness—as the true gate to Hades was revealed to the world.

18

"Stop!" Xena shouted, and crouched low.

Lightning-quick, a rusty metal spike shot out of the wall, piercing the air where her head had been only a second before.

Xena grabbed the razor-tipped spike and yanked herself up, pulling her feet up just as another metal bar sprang from the wall at knee level.

Xena jerked her head to the left, saw where the next would shoot out, and straightened her arms. Her head tapped the ceiling as she pitched forward and rolled herself over the top spike—

—as the third burst out, aimed at a standing man's stomach.

Xena dropped to the other side, in front of the trio of deadly weapons. She turned and saw that Gabrielle and Alesandra hadn't been hurt—although both were pale and shaking.

Gabrielle started to speak, but her voice was drowned out by a horrible, rending moan from somewhere close by, a bizarre cry that echoed and rang through the dark hallway. The very foundation of the castle trembled with the terrible sound, and Xena felt her heart begin to thump anxiously.

"Quickly," said Xena, and they stooped over, wriggling between the rusty bars to join her.

Xena took off down the hall at a dead run, pulling the others behind her. That was the last trap—it had to be—and if it wasn't, too bad—a quick death might be better, if that cry belonged to their opponent.

From the sound of it, Bain had discovered what he was looking for.

Beyond the wall was a giant hallway, stretching back into shadows that flickered and danced with a deep, murky light. From off in the distance, Telius could hear the cries from his childhood imaginings, the restless, tortured screams of those cursed to remain in Hades—but he barely heard them; he was too entranced by the monstrous beast that snarled and pawed at the ground in front of him.

Cerebrus was huge, three times the size of a normal dog, its dark body thickly muscled and powerful. From its barrel chest sprang three stout necks, topped with three angry and evil faces, their metallic teeth snapping and growling. Six red-rimmed eyes glared at Telius, the long jaws of each head like a wolf's jaws, lean and efficient for their killing purpose. Foam dripped down from each chin, the snouts quivering, taking in Telius's scent.

The middle head of Cerebrus dropped back, howling to the skies, and the other two joined it, the combined noise worse than any nightmare, filling the chamber with the sound of death.

They stopped their cry, and the beast lunged forward, snarling—

—but was held back, as if by an invisible chain. Cerebrus lunged again, but could not come any closer than where the stone wall had been. It was a creature of Hades, and could not leave its post.

Telius gazed at it in wonder and fear, astounded by its very existence, forgetting for a moment everything that he had planned. This was Cerebrus, the guard of the gate!

The animal snapped and whined in fury,

trying desperately to get at him. It could not, and that denial seemed to fire its rage to even greater heights, the beast insane in its desire to reach him, to rip him to shreds in its horrible jaws.

Gods, if only Father could see *this—*

The thought of Martus broke his trance, reminding him of his incredible purpose. With a final look at the slavering creature, Telius dropped his gaze to the ritual, having forgotten the three words that would slay the keeper of the gate.

"Sacritil! Zeniphous! *Amithese!*"

As he shouted the final word, he heard a cry from behind him.

"No! *Wait!*"

Telius spun, saw two women and a little girl, but *how did they get in?*

He turned back—*it doesn't matter now*—readying himself for the death of the monster—

—and felt his stomach plummet, his knees suddenly weak with terror.

As the terrible Cerebrus broke from its invisible chain and, snarling ferociously, entered the room in which they stood.

Muscle memory. Without a thought, Xena drew her sword and ran to meet the raging beast.

If Cerebrus knew fear, there was no sign—the dog leapt at her, each of its jaws straining and gnashing to tear at her throat.

Xena slashed, left-right, cleanly slicing through the dark and muscled necks of two of the howling heads. A blood as deep red as to be almost black immediately started to flow, staining the giant chest of the creature—

—and those heads fell back and bayed, a long and deeply angry sound of pain and fury. But even as Xena watched, and the dog leapt backward shrieking, knocking over guttering candles and stacks of old books—the wounds began to *heal*, the cuts mending right before her eyes, the tissue knitting over to close the deep gashes.

Xena raised her sword and the dog growled, its many red eyes filled with blood lust—but it didn't lunge at her again. Her flashing blade had given Cerebrus something to be wary of, and the creature glared at her but circled back slowly.

As she followed along with the movement of the beast, she felt an amazing and horrible sensation behind her—coming from deep within the corridor that glowed with hidden fires—a great wave of oppressive blackness, a feeling and not a vision, seemed to press out

191

from the entrance to Hades. It was as if an invisible wall of every bad feeling under the sun had come together and was pushing to be free of the netherworld.

Even as Xena realized what this meant, Alesandra shouted out from somewhere behind her.

"Don't kill it, Xena! It keeps the souls in, but also the darkness!"

Xena didn't acknowledge the information; she was too busy watching the monstrosity in front of her as its wounds mended and it prepared itself to attack again, rumbling throatily. She could see its intention in the way it watched her, the way it circled, its muscles tensing in anticipation.

But the prophet's words were true—she could feel the wall of despair and hatred pressing against her, almost a physical sensation it was so strong. To kill it would be to release the tortured souls of Hades, yes—but also the evil. Every cruelty that was trapped in the darkness beyond that hallway would be loosed upon the world; the souls of those that had only become *more* murderous in captivity would be free to roam. The prophecy would come into being.

Then how to stop it? If she couldn't kill

it, there had to be a way to leash it once again . . .

Xena's eyes widened—what had Alesandra said before, about Bain's intentions? To "undo" the beast? Xena had assumed that Bain had meant to kill it, but the wording was deceptive—and thank Gods that whatever he'd done, he had not succeeded in the creature's death! Then there would have been nothing keeping the horrors of Hades from getting out!

Bain *had* undone Cerebrus, probably thinking that Hades would fall without its guard—but it had been a terrible mistake. He had only broken whatever bond had kept the monster leashed to its post. And if the beast escaped . . .

Xena shouted over the dog's renewed howls of anger, still circling.

"Find the spell that will return it to where it was! You must find the spell—"

She was cut off by the monster's sudden movement, the giant dog tired of prolonging the fight. With a scream like the loathsome soul of Hades itself, Cerebrus leapt forward.

Telius had jumped back as Cerebrus broke its invisible chain, and the warrior woman rushed forward to battle it. His shock could not have been any greater if the ceiling had opened up and rained gold.

Why isn't it dead? Who *were* these people, how had they—

A girl. A warrior. Wait.

The truth was there, spoken in his father's voice—the dream! The painting of Martus that day in the main corridor, it had been a warning—and he *hadn't listened*!

Telius turned wild and frightened eyes to the girl-child as she cried out to the warrior. "Don't kill it, Xena! It keeps the souls in, but also the darkness!"

He reeled from the words, suddenly knowing them to be the truth. He could *feel* it now, the sensation of spite and hatred that fairly projected out from the dim corridor that led to Hades's gate. What had he *done?* How could he have been so blind?

He cursed himself, cursed his impatience and his stupidity. In his desperate need to prove himself worthy of his father's name, he had risked—

Everyone. Everything.

He could barely fathom the reality of what he might have done, the implications of his actions. Even as he fought to deny the truth that welled up inside of him, he knew that there could be no escape from it.

He, Telius, son of Martus Bain, may have sentenced them all to a world of pain and suffering.

Gabrielle watched in horror as the wounds that Xena had inflicted miraculously began to close and heal. She heard Alesandra shout for Xena not to kill the creature, but watching those cuts mend themselves, she wondered if it was even *possible* to destroy the thing.

Xena didn't look away from the snarling dog as she cried out, her words almost lost in the clamor of the beast.

"Find the spell that will return it! You must find the spell—"

Cerebrus suddenly lunged forward, and Xena jumped to the side, and slammed the hilt of her sword into the side of one of the terrible heads.

The dog yelped and turned, snapping—

—and Xena hit it again, dancing forward and then back nimbly, the hilt clunking dully against the skull of one shrieking head, then another.

Cerebrus staggered back in frustration and pain, and Gabrielle finally allowed herself to hear what Xena had shouted.

—*must find the spell*—

Gabrielle reached out and grabbed the arm

195

of the young man nearby, jerking him around to face her.

"The spell, the ritual! How do we undo it?"

He gazed at her blankly. "What? I don't—"

His dark eyes seemed far away, his skin pale and sickly. He was in shock, useless.

Gabrielle watched as Cerebrus lunged at Xena again, howling—and what she saw next chilled her heart, made her cry out in fear and surprise.

Xena threw down her sword in the clutter of shredded books and dead candles—and faced the frenzied monster unarmed.

19

Xena realized that if she kept the sword, Cerebrus would be killed. The thought flashed through her mind in a split second, as the baying, snapping beast lunged forward again, and she saw the opening—one swift thrust to the heart, and Cerebrus would be no more, the legends of invincibility proved wrong—

No!

She threw down the weapon before she changed her mind. Her blood was high, her actions hardly thought out, and she knew that in the heat of battle, she might not be able to stop herself from delivering the killing stroke. *Cerebrus must not die.*

Even as her sword clattered to the stone floor, Cerebus lunged again. She jumped and spun, and landed just behind the creature;

two of its heads craned around, and then all of them roared out, frustrated with this fruitless attack. It turned and charged again.

"The spell!" Xena shouted once more, and dove into a shoulder roll as the huge dog pounced. Their only hope was to reverse the damage done—and she had to keep Cerebrus distracted until the others found the way.

Hurry, she thought, and jumped again as the talons of the creature dug furrows in the stone, clawing for her blood.

Gabrielle grabbed at the young man again, digging her fingers into his shoulders. "We have to find a way to undo the spell!"

"Undo the beast," he said, and stared at her with those blank eyes. "Undone. My father is undone, and he was so good . . ."

Gabrielle released him, her mind a solid whirl of terror and frustration. The guy was no longer part of this reality; the shock had undone *him*. What could they *do*?

Alesandra was still beside her, watching the battle with horrified eyes. Gabrielle stared at her, grasping for a solution—

Avernus!

It all clicked into place at once. Xena had *known* how to find the lake, but it had taken

Alesandra's gift to find the truth inside of the warrior—

"Alesandra! Touch him! Touch Bain! Find the spell!"

The child turned to her and her brown eyes flashed in understanding. She ran forward and snatched for Bain's hand, grasping at the man's cold fingers and closing her eyes.

Gabrielle turned, just in time to see Cerebrus reach out with one mighty claw—

—and rake down Xena's arm, drawing blood.

Xena sprang back, but too late. Cerebrus's ragged talons had found the bare flesh of her arm, digging through the skin.

She instantly dampened the pain—there was no time—and quickly cataloged the wound. Not deep, no scars, bearable—

Cerebrus howled in gleeful victory, its snouts quivering at the scent of fresh blood, and it lashed out again, eager to draw more.

"Not this time," breathed Xena, and she ducked the giant claw, bent down—and delivered a powerful side-kick to its chest. A rib snapped.

Cerebrus screamed and backed away, whining. Xena touched her own wound, reaffirming to herself that it wasn't too bad, and then crouched, ready for the next attack. She was running out of breath, and out of strength; she wouldn't be able to hold the creature off for too much longer.

They had to find the spell soon, or the prophecy of darkness would be fulfilled.

Telius watched blankly as the little girl took his hand and closed her eyes. He wanted only to lie down somewhere and go to sleep, somewhere away from all this noise and these people he didn't know—

His fingers tingled, and he felt a strange thing; memories flashed through his mind, so quickly that he only caught bits and pieces of the thoughts—spells, incantations, things that he'd read and forgotten . . .

Memories of his father, of lessons on sorcery. Of the need to be careful, ever so wary of magic and its consequences, to know without doubt the results of spells before practicing them.

Telius felt his eyes fill with tears. He had been so foolish! He had ignored a lifetime of teachings and tried to take the easy way, using a spell that he knew nothing about—

He blinked, suddenly aware of where he was and what was happening. He stared down at the child, and felt the great gift that she held, that she used now, searching for an answer to the horror that he had created.

Telius closed his eyes, grateful, and helped her look. *A spell of reversal,* he thought, hoping that it would give her something to work with.

Her fingers tightened against his, and he knew that she had heard him. Maybe she could find a solution in his tired mind, a ritual that would set right what he had done.

If she didn't, they would all die, and the rest of humanity would pay for his mistake.

Cerebrus's broken rib must have healed. Its whines had become growls again, and its heads ducked low, barking and hissing at Xena.

Xena backed away, heart hammering from exertion. The dog jumped, and Xena danced, whirling and spinning, darting away from the slashing jaws. Her dance was true, all of her instincts in full play, feinting left and right as the dog snapped and howled, torn pages of ancient books flying up around their legs.

Cerebrus suddenly seemed to grin, the look in its eyes somehow sly, cunningly calculating as it watched her. The dog spun and stepped into the huge, shadow-filled corridor that led out of the chamber, turning back to face her again with all of its terrible eyes. It barked, backing into the hallway, trying to get her to follow.

Xena instinctively took a step forward, ready to battle, and then stopped, and frowned. The realization hit her like a cold slap across the face—if she set foot in that passage, she would be lost. The gate was too near, and she would fall in to that oppressive darkness, never to step out again.

"Nice try," she panted, and stood there, waiting. If the dog wanted to stand in the hall, let it—all the more time for the others to find the spell.

Cerebrus must have seen that she would not follow. It crouched and tensed, and with a killing roar, it sprang forward once again.

Alesandra opened her eyes. "I've got it!"

Bain nodded excitedly, letting go of her hand. Gabrielle had watched their silent search urgently, praying for them to hurry, turning often to look on in horror at the strange battle between Xena and the monstrous dog-thing.

"Where?"

Alesandra looked at her in fear. "*There,*" she said heavily, and pointed. "It's big, leather-bound."

Gabrielle's heart sank. Alesandra was pointing at a scattered pile of books only a dozen paces away—and right in between Xena and the lunging beast.

Gabrielle took a deep breath and steeled herself, trying not to think of what she was about to do. If she thought about it, she wouldn't be able to, *couldn't*—

"Stay here," she said, and without a backward glance, she crouched and ran, falling to her knees amid the scattered books.

"Gabrielle, *no!*"

Xena heard Alesandra's cry, but didn't dare turn away from the deadly Cerebrus. Again, it raised its gleaming talons and stabbed at her, howling. She jumped, let the claws rip through air—

—and suddenly Gabrielle was there, on the floor, scrabbling through the shredded books *right in front of Cerebrus*—

"Hey!" Xena shouted, and the dog looked up, away from Gabrielle—as Xena vaulted herself over her friend and crashed into the surprised creature, knocking it back.

The warrior, Xena, had exhibited bravery like none Telius had ever seen, leaping straight at the beast to protect the young woman—

"Here!" the blonde shouted, holding up an oversized book, bound in leather. She jumped to her feet and pulled back, aiming—

As she threw the book, Cerebrus lunged forward, the warrior clinging to its giant back, beating at one barking head with her bare fists. To no avail.

Even as the book flew through the air, the mighty dog swung one powerful neck from side to side, whacking the young blond woman's head and driving her to the floor.

From where she didn't rise again.

"No!"

Xena screamed as she saw Gabrielle go down, crumpling to the floor in a heap.

She jumped from the dog, scooped up Gabrielle, and was away in only a second. Gabrielle didn't move in her arms.

Xena set her down quickly, away from the grinning Cerebrus, and felt her heart turn to ice and ashes, all at once. She saw her sword, gleaming from the floor, and scooped it up, her eyes blazing with a fury she had never felt in all her years as a fighter.

With a howl that surpassed the rage of the creature, she sprang forward, ready to kill.

•   •   •

Telius caught the book in a fumbling motion and turned to the girl. The child reached out and took the book from him, flipping through the pages rapidly.

"This one!"

She handed him the book, and Telius scanned it quickly—yes, he remembered this, a simple spell that reversed a spoken incantation—

He started to read, speaking rapidly. "All this that hath gone through, know these words to break the taken thrall—"

"Xena, no, you *can't*!"

Telius didn't look up as the child cried out; whatever the child had seen, Telius knew that they were almost out of time.

He read faster, feeling the power of the spell fill him up.

Xena slashed at the monster, nothing held back. Nothing would satisfy her but to see it dead.

Gabrielle! Her mind cried out, and she let the pain guide her sword, driving Cerebrus back. The dog howled and snapped, but Xena felt no fear. She cut, sliced, drew blood from its throats, from its legs and heads.

It fell back farther, whining now, stumbling. Still she slashed, drawing new blood for each cut that healed. Alesandra shouted for her to stop, but the vision of Gabrielle's crumpled body fed her rage, urging her on.

The man, Bain, was shouting, too, but his words made no sense to her. Nothing mattered; Gabrielle could be dead, and Cerebrus would pay for it.

Time had no meaning as she danced forward, her movements quick and sure. There was only her sword and her dance, and the imminent death of the thing in front of her. She blinked, and the dog had somehow been backed into the far corner of the room. It snarled at her, still whining, but Xena could see that it needed time now to heal itself; it would not attack.

She raised her sword, aiming for the dog's foul black heart, ready to put an end to this monster that had hurt, maybe *killed* her dearest friend—

—and then she stopped, the sword quivering in her upraised hands. Gabrielle, her dearest friend . . .

Who had traveled with her to halt the prophecy.

Who had wanted nothing more than to keep the evils of Hades from being loosed.

Whose life didn't deserve to be connected

to the death of Cerebrus—and consequently, the freedom of Hades's evil.

Xena lowered her weapon slowly, feeling the strange trance of her fury break and crumble. She backed away from the injured creature, watching as it licked its wounds with three tongues and tiredly got to its feet, growling with pain.

From behind her, she heard a sweet and beautiful sound that made her want to cry out in joy and relief.

"Xena? What happened?"

She turned, and saw a groggy Gabrielle sitting up, rubbing at her head. Xena's heart suddenly seemed to beat again, as if it had gone still throughout her vicious battle—and she smiled, stepping toward her friend.

Gabrielle's eyes widened. "Look out!"

Xena spun. As Cerebrus leapt for her with death in its eyes.

"Look out!"

Telius read the final words. ". . . and will be no more!"

He looked up, just in time to see the monster dog jump straight for the warrior, a lunge that would certainly kill her—

—and then, suddenly, there was no Cerebrus. No corridor.

Only a wall, etched with languages long dead, the last wisps of a strange, gray mist curling away at the corners. Only a flood of shredded books—and two women and a little girl, all laughing at once, running to one another and embracing.

It was over.

20

As the moon rose high and full over the Castle Bain, they told their stories.

The four of them sat in the kitchen, the three travelers enjoying their first decent meal in a week. Gabrielle had gone out and fetched Argos, and Bain had been happy to tell them—over big glasses of fresh milk and plates of cold roasted chicken—that he kept a good stock of horseshoes on hand. They could fit Argos in the morning, and he insisted that they allow him to restock their meager supplies, as well. Xena accepted, nodding her approval.

After Telius had told them his tale, Xena had come to see him as Alesandra had in her vision; truly, he had no evil in his heart. He was young, and had suffered the foolhardy confidence of too little experience—but she could see that he had learned his lesson, however brutal the experience had been.

Alesandra had taken to him immediately, perhaps because of his open acceptance of her gift. He looked at her with admiration, impressed by the depth of her powers, and Alesandra was obviously delighted with his open respect for her abilities. Xena could also see that Alesandra connected with him on another, deeper level—she had lost Otus and Telius had lost his own father, both recently. The child took his hand as he described the passing of Martus, and Xena saw how touched Telius was by the gesture.

Gabrielle was quite pleased with herself, and kept reaching up to touch the lump that had risen beneath her scalp where Cerebrus had whacked it; an admirable war wound, to say the least. The prophecy had been stopped, and she had played an important role, just as Alesandra had predicted. All of them had—without one another, they would have lost the war to Hades.

Telius had already apologized a dozen times, and now started to again.

"I can't tell you how grateful I am that you all came; if I hadn't been so stupid—"

Xena held up her bandaged arm. "Please.

What matters is that you've seen your mistake."

Telius nodded. "Perhaps I'll try again—in twenty or thirty years, after I've studied a *lot* more."

He turned to Alesandra and smiled at her. "Maybe you could come back sometime and learn *with* me. Your powers are great, and I could really benefit from someone who could tell me which spells might be harmful . . ."

Alesandra's eyes shone. "Really?"

Telius nodded. "And I could teach you more about your gifts. There are so many books here on prophecy, I can't even count them all."

Xena and Gabrielle exchanged a glance, and Xena grinned. She didn't need second sight to know that *all* of Alesandra's vision was about to come true. The child would not be leaving the castle with them after all, but not for the reasons they had feared.

Alesandra had found a place that she could call home.

Xena slept late for a change, and awoke feeling refreshed. Her wounded arm was already itching beneath the bandages, a sure sign that the flesh was on the mend.

She walked out of the comfortable guest

chamber she had stayed in and leaned around the open entryway of the room next door, smiling at the sound of Gabrielle's light snore. She briefly considered waking her up with the promise of something disgusting for breakfast, but decided to let her sleep a little longer; she deserved it.

Xena wandered back down to the kitchen, marveling along the way at the design of the castle, and found Telius and Alesandra already laughing together over a morning meal.

"Xena! Telius has asked me if I want to stay here!"

Xena smiled. "Do you?"

The child searched Xena's gaze with her own. "Is that okay? I mean, would you . . . mind?"

Xena shook her head. "I think that sounds wonderful. I'm very happy for you, for both of you."

Alesandra jumped up and ran to her, hugging her around the waist. "And he says it's okay if Binjer comes to live here, too!"

Xena cocked an eyebrow at Telius. "Really?"

Telius grinned. "Yes, and I know what I'm getting into. I remember him from when he came before, a long time ago."

Xena smiled. "He's hard to forget."

Alesandra looked up her, her eyes bright with happiness, and Xena found herself surprised by the warmth of emotion she felt from the girl, and for her.

The warrior dropped to her knees and returned Alesandra's embrace.

By noon, Argos was laden with several stuffed packs of supplies and treats, and sported a full new set of shoes. The four of them stood just outside the castle gate, saying their good-byes.

Alesandra hugged Gabrielle for the hundredth time, making her promise once again that she and Xena would visit soon.

"We will, really," said Gabrielle, and smiled at Telius over Alesandra's head. Telius grinned back, and Gabrielle found herself a little bit flustered at the look in his dark eyes and the beauty of his smile. It was obvious that she would be welcomed by *both* of them, for very different reasons.

Not too shabby, thought Gabrielle, and she smiled wider. She could do a whole lot worse, that was for sure. Of course, Xena needed her, for now; they had adventures to find, and battles to fight. But that didn't mean she couldn't take a *vacation* every now and then . . .

Xena mounted Argos, smiling to herself at the obvious glances being swapped back and forth between Telius and Gabrielle. She had the feeling that Gabrielle would be hinting about another trip to Avernus before too long . . .

Alesandra stepped back from Gabrielle, still holding her hands, and giggled, looking back over her shoulder at Telius, her honeyed eyes glowing.

"You're right," she whispered loudly, and both Gabrielle and Telius blushed, realizing that Alesandra had picked up a bit more than a simple hug. Suddenly they both developed an active interest in looking anywhere but at each other.

"The first thing you learn is *tact*," said Telius good-naturedly, and put an arm around the giggling Alesandra.

Xena tactfully changed the subject herself. "We should reach Binjer in less than a week, so expect him in two—assuming that he doesn't have too many belongings to pack."

Alesandra nodded. "Two weeks, that's about right; I *told* you he was going to move soon."

"Thank you, Xena, Gabrielle," said Telius, raising his hand in farewell. He'd never be able to repay them for all they had done, but raising Alesandra in a happy home might be a start. Already, he had come to care about the child, and knew that they could learn a lot from each other.

"I'll never forget you," said Alesandra, her voice a husky whisper. "You believed in me, and I love you, both of you . . ."

Gabrielle felt a rising lump in her throat and swallowed it down. "We love you, too," she said, and Xena nodded.

"Be good," the warrior added, and fixed Telius with a mock-stern gaze. "*Both* of you."

Their gentle laughter ushered the travelers on their way, Gabrielle walking alongside Argos.

After a mile or so, Gabrielle looked up at Xena. "What are we going to do, after we find Binjer?"

Xena shrugged. "I don't know. I thought we could head east for a while, see if we can manage to stay out of trouble for a week or two."

Gabrielle grinned playfully. "What, you're tired of saving the world already?"

Xena sighed dramatically. "A woman's work is *never* done, Gabrielle." Then she grinned back at her friend.

Together, pleased with themselves and the world, they made their way through a bright and sunny day.

Xena, Warrior Princess

A novel by
RU EMERSON

Based on the hit television series created by
John Schulian and Robert Tapert

Xena, once in love with conquest and destruction,
now fights for the side of good. Though constantly
haunted by her wicked past, Xena courageously
battles mortals, gods, demigods and monsters, and
heroically protects the downtrodden from the
forces of evil.

The Empty Throne

In a small, remote village, Xena and her protégé,
Gabrielle, make a stunning discovery: all of the
men in town have disappeared without a trace.
Meanwhile, armed bands are running rampant in
the streets. What mysterious and malevolent force
is at work? Strange magic? Godly might? Xena and
Gabrielle must uncover the truth before it is *their*
turn to disappear . . .

ISBN 0 00 651150 3

Xena, Warrior Princess

A novel by
RU EMERSON

Based on the hit television series created by
John Schulian and Robert Tapert

Xena, once in love with conquest and destruction, now fights for the side of good. Though constantly haunted by her wicked past, Xena courageously battles mortals, gods, demigods and monsters, and heroically protects the downtrodden from the forces of evil.

The Huntress
and the Sphinx

No one is braver or faster than the legendary huntress, Atalanta. Or so *she* says. And when Xena and Gabrielle are asked to rescue a group of kidnapped children, Atalanta is the first to volunteer. After all, she is the only one who could possibly be strong enough to succeed. But when they find the kidnapper, Xena realizes that no one is strong enough to defeat it. For who can challenge the power and the knowledge of the almighty Sphinx?

ISBN 0 00 651115 1

Xena, Warrior Princess

A novel by
RU EMERSON

Based on the hit television series created by
John Schulian and Robert Tapert

Xena, once in love with conquest and destruction, now fights for the side of good. Though constantly haunted by her wicked past, Xena courageously battles mortals, gods, demigods and monsters, and heroically protects the downtrodden from the forces of evil.

The Thief of Hermes

His name is like Helarion, fleet of foot, full of charm and a thief like no other. He claims to be the son of Hermes, the Sun god and divine trickster. When he frames Xena and Gabrielle for one of his crimes, they must plan a daring jailbreak – and suddenly they are living like true cutpurses. Is Helarion good or evil? A god's child or a liar? Xena and Gabrielle don't have time to find out. For they're about the be drawn into an adventure only the son of Hermes could survive . . .

ISBN 0 00 651152 X